"Hello, Missy."

Missy stepped back as if she'd seen a ghost, but then, he imagined, she had. "Jonas," she whispered, putting a hand to her chest as if a bullet had pierced her heart. Pure shock, nothing more. "You're supposed to be dead."

"Better late than never," he mumbled as the adrenaline he'd been running on finally fizzled. His legs fell out from under him. He hit the wall, keeled over and collapsed onto the porch floor.

"Jonas? Jonas." Her hands touched his chest. Nice, soft hands. Hands that spread warmth all the way to his limbs. Hands he'd dreamed of more than he cared to remember.

Dear Reader,

I can't believe this is already the fourth in the Mirabelle series. It seems like just yesterday I was writing about Sophie and Noah, and Mirabelle's islanders were still a mystery to me.

When Missy first appeared in Garrett and Erica's story, I had no clue she'd once been married. But when Natalie came to the island in the third Mirabelle book, Missy's story started taking shape. Trust me. Jonas was as much a surprise to me as he was to Missy. That timing thing really does make life interesting!

My next book, due out in November, is Kate Dillon's story. Some of you might remember her as the feisty younger sister in *Finding Mr. Right*. She and a certain bodyguard have some issues to figure out and it should be fun!

And with any luck you'll have three more Mirabelle stories to look forward to in 2011. I think Sarah is due for her own story, don't you?

I love hearing from readers, and I answer all correspondence. So drop me an e-mail at helenbrenna@comcast.net, or send your letter to P.O. Box 24107, Minneapolis, MN 55424.

My best,

Helen Brenna

Along Came a Husband
Helen Brenna

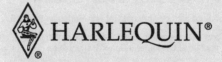

HARLEQUIN®

TORONTO • NEW YORK • LONDON
AMSTERDAM • PARIS • SYDNEY • HAMBURG
STOCKHOLM • ATHENS • TOKYO • MILAN • MADRID
PRAGUE • WARSAW • BUDAPEST • AUCKLAND

Recycling programs
for this product may
not exist in your area.

ISBN-13: 978-0-373-71640-1

ALONG CAME A HUSBAND

www.eHarlequin.com

Printed in U.S.A.

ABOUT THE AUTHOR

Helen Brenna grew up in a small town in central Minnesota, the seventh of eight children. Although she never dreamed of writing books, she's always been a voracious reader of romances. So after taking a break from her accounting career, she tried her hand at writing the romances she loves to read. Since her first book was published in 2007, she's won a prestigious Romance Writers of America RITA® Award, an *RT Book Reviews* Reviewer's Choice award and a Virginia Romance Writers' HOLT Medallion. Helen still lives in Minnesota with her husband, two children and far too many pets. She'd love to hear from you. E-mail her at helenbrenna@comcast.net or send mail to P.O. Box 24107, Minneapolis, MN 55424. Visit her Web site at www.helenbrenna.com or chat with Helen and other authors at RidingWithTheTopDown.blogspot.com.

Books by Helen Brenna

HARLEQUIN SUPERROMANCE

1403—TREASURE
1425—DAD FOR LIFE
1519—FINDING MR. RIGHT
1582—FIRST COME TWINS*
1594—NEXT COMES LOVE*
1606—THEN COMES BABY*

*An Island to Remember

HARLEQUIN NASCAR

PEAK PERFORMANCE
FROM THE OUTSIDE

For Mary Kuryla, my big sis, who never lets me forget she changed my diapers.

I love you!

Acknowledgments

As usual, I had no plot when I started writing this story. Thank you, thank you, thank you Chris Lashinski and Roxanne Richardson for your brainstorming ideas, critiques, encouragement and, above all, friendship. I could, possibly, do this without you, but it wouldn't be half as much fun.

Once again, heartfelt thanks to my neighbor, George Kyrilis, for his expertise in all things FBI. America is a safer place because of people like you.

Thanks for your service, George!

Thanks to Tracy Dickovich, a very special person who showed me firsthand the benefits of healing touch massage. Are you sure you don't have eight hands?

And I can't forget my agent, Tina Wexler, on this one. Thank you, dear, for helping make Missy and Jonas's story better and better!

You guys are the best!

CHAPTER ONE

"I'VE ALWAYS LOVED A GOOD thunderstorm," Missy Charms murmured as lightning crackled outside the front windows of her gift shop and thunder rumbled over the roof of the historic brick building. "There's nothing like early summer rain to settle the heat and wash away the dust and grime."

"So says the quintessential earth child." Sarah Marshik jumped as another bolt of lightning momentarily brightened the early evening sky. "Me? I can't stand 'em."

"I think they're cool." Brian, Sarah's young son, went to stand beside Missy near the front of the store.

Together, they peered through the droplet-spattered windows overlooking the center of Mirabelle Island's old-world quaintness. Other than an odd tourist or two caught unprepared in the sudden downpour and running from under one green-and-white awning to the next, the cobblestone streets were deserted. Slim, the black, short-haired cat Missy had rescued many years ago, rubbed against her leg, and she scooped him up.

Another bright and fiery flash lit the sky, and Brian grinned at Missy. "That was awesome!"

"Totally. It means we're going to have lots of wind tonight," she predicted, scratching the cat's ears. "And a hotter than normal summer."

"How do you know?" Brian asked, his eyes wide and round and oh, so innocent.

"I just know." She winked. Where would be the fun in explaining her predictions came straight from Zuni weather lore?

"Missy can predict the future," Sarah said, grinning.

"Tell my future!" Brian held out his hand. "Read my palm. Please, please, please!"

Missy glared good-naturedly at Sarah. Sarah may have beaten Missy to Mirabelle by a few months, but it seemed the two had been destined to become best friends. Not only were their businesses located side by side on Main Street, but, most important, they'd both seemed lost in the world. That is, before they'd found Mirabelle and each other.

"Bri, hon," Missy said, shaking her head, "no one can tell the future from someone's palm." She'd learned that the hard way.

"You can. I've heard you talking about it with Mom. There's a life line and a line that tells you how rich you're going to be and—"

"Okay, already." Missy laughed. Setting Slim back down, she took the little boy's hand and ran her fingers along his palm, pretending to concentrate. "I see...hmm, that's interesting."

"What? What?"

"Oh, she's pretty."

"A girl? I don't want to know about girls." He cringed. "I wanna know if I'm going to be a pitcher for the Twins."

"Baseball?" She shook her head. "Trust me. Love's more important."

Brian pulled back his hand and rolled his eyes. "*Nothing's* more important than baseball."

"If only that would last." Sarah shook her head. "Do you want us to stay and visit with you while you eat?"

Given the bad weather, Sarah had only one or two customers shopping for flowers the entire day, so she'd closed up a little early to be with Brian. As the island wedding planner, Sarah was smack-dab in the middle of her busiest time of the year. Even so, knowing Missy was stuck alone in her store until closing, she'd dropped off a tomato mozzarella salad from Duffy's Pub.

"You and Bri take off," Missy said. "I don't want you to be late for your movie."

"You'll be okay here?"

"It'll be quiet." She smiled. "A good night to get some things done."

She could make several chakra bracelets or dust a few shelves or simply sit and enjoy the thunderstorm with a cup of herbal tea. It would be lonely, but Missy had grown used to being alone. At least that's what she told herself every day. She glanced at Brian and the ache that had steadily grown stronger over the past several years pierced her heart like a jagged spear.

As if Sarah had read Missy's thoughts, she gently touched her son on the shoulder. "Brian, go use Missy's bathroom before we take off." After the little boy had dashed toward the rear of the store, Sarah cautiously asked, "Any news on the adoption front?"

More than anything in the world Missy wanted a child, but it seemed the one thing in the world she couldn't make happen. For now she'd have to settle for Slim. As if sensing her sudden turn of emotion, the cat wove himself around her legs. Slim may have had free rein of Mirabelle, running in and out of his kitty doors at will, but he usually chose to stick by her side.

"Actually." Missy picked up the cat again. Holding him, petting his soft fur, always calmed her. "Barbara called earlier today to tell me she's hopeful about a new match."

"That's great! Why didn't you say something earlier?"

Because Missy's representative at the adoption agency had been *hopeful* about the past five matches and they, too, had gone absolutely nowhere. Years ago, after the agency had explained that a stable, safe, supportive community would be essential, Missy had decided to settle here on the island. How could there be a better place on this earth to raise a child than Mirabelle? But, as it turned out, place hadn't been enough to tip the adoption scales in favor of a single young woman.

"I was afraid I'd jinx the deal by getting my hopes up," Missy said softly, unable to keep the disappointment from her voice.

"Maybe you should reconsider the alternatives?"

After a great deal of thought, Missy had decided to go the private adoption route. She'd finally found the right agency, filled out all the necessary applications and paperwork, and gone through the grueling home study process. "I'm not switching horses midstream."

"I'm talking about the old-fashioned route. You know. Man, woman, marriage, child."

"Not an option." Missy shook her head. "I met the one true love of my life, and we both know how that turned out." She believed in Fate changing lives, always had, but over the years she'd come to accept that every once in a while Fate managed to screw up.

"Well, there's a certain someone on the island who seems darned close to wanting you to reconsider."

Sean Griffin. Sarah had to be referring to the new doctor. "We're friends, Sarah. That's all."

"Well, if Natalie can do it," Sarah said, giving Missy a quick hug, "so can you."

Natalie, their friend who ran a summer camp for disadvantaged kids on the northwest end of the island, had adopted four adolescents this past winter *before* she'd married Jamis. Although Missy preferring a baby or young child made her chances for adoption more difficult, their friend's success as a single woman had given Missy the first real hope she'd had in years.

Brian came running through the store. "Come on, Mom. Let's go."

Missy grabbed her raincoat from the back of the chair by the cash register and held it out toward Sarah. "Why don't you take my slicker?"

"You'll need it when you go home."

"I don't mind getting wet. Besides, I think it's supposed to clear up for a while before another band of storms comes through." As Missy held open the front door to her shop, she took in a deep lungful of air. And frowned.

Something wasn't right.

She glanced out the windows with a partial view of Lake Superior. Beyond the marina, waves crashed against the breakwater and sprayed into the air. Down the rocky coast, turbulent water hit the shoreline with damaging strength. The clouds in the early evening sky boiled and churned, shifted by an unseen but powerful force.

Sarah shrugged on the rain slicker and glanced at Missy. "You all right? You look like you've seen a ghost."

"I'm fine." Missy swallowed, trying to compose herself. "I'll be fine."

"Okay, then." Sarah stepped partway through the door and grabbed Brian's hand. "See you at lunch tomorrow." Then she took off down the wet sidewalk.

"Bye, Missy!" Brian called as he followed his mom.

"Bye, Bri!" Missy said absently as she watched the flower baskets hanging from the black lampposts swing and sway in the storm. The wind chimes hanging near her gift shop entrance jangled fiercely in a sudden gust, and an uneasy feeling settled in the pit of her stomach.

Something was in the air out there that had nothing to do with a cleansing rain, or a possible adoption match, or the droves of happy tourists already flocking daily to Mirabelle for long-awaited summer vacations and holidays. This was bitter and acidic. Unexpected. Fierce. And it was blowing Missy's way.

"You TELLING ME I CAN'T GET to Mirabelle Island tonight?" Jonas Abel glared at the clerk on the other side of the locked glass door as lightning flared a short distance down the Lake Superior shoreline.

"That's not what I said."

It had been raining most of the day. Jonas's clothes were damp and cold and clinging to his skin and all he wanted was to be warm and dry. Entirely off the grid was the objective, but at the moment that appeared to be asking for too much.

"It isn't even eleven yet, and I missed the last ferry?" Jonas grumbled. "What kind of backwoods place is this?" On a few select streets in Chicago, he might've gotten away with pointing a gun at the old man's head, but not in this world.

"See there?" The old man motioned toward the schedule mounted on the outside of the ferry building. "During June, the last ferry to the island leaves Bayfield at 10 p.m. Won't be another one 'til morning. Now on the weekends, it's eleven. And during July—"

"I don't give a damn about July." He clenched his teeth against the intense pain in his side. "I need to get to Mirabelle tonight."

"No need to get huffy with me. Can't wait 'til morning, you can always hire a water taxi."

A car rolled into the wet parking lot, and Jonas instinctively drew his soggy hood over his head. As the vehicle cruised through a puddle and under the light of a nearby lamppost, he slipped his good hand inside his sweatshirt, gripping his gun, and studied the occupants.

Teenage boy. Girlfriend. In love.

Good luck with that.

He turned back toward the old man. "I need a water taxi." Leaning against the door frame, he struggled to stay alert. Although it was impossible anyone could've followed Jonas here, he'd do best to get out of sight. "Can you help me?"

Half an hour later, a sprinkling of rain stinging his cheeks, he was on a boat speeding across the choppy black waters of Lake Superior and closing in on the shoreline of what he assumed was Mirabelle. Lights twinkled in the darkness outlining a concentration of buildings near the marina, most likely houses dotting the hillside and what looked like a large hotel on the outskirts of town. By the time the boat docked at the dimly lit pier, it was so dark Jonas could barely tell water from shore.

"There you go." The taxi driver flipped his engine into neutral and glanced at Jonas. "You okay? You don't look so good."

"I'm fine." Somehow Jonas made it onto the dock. He dragged his heavy pack over his shoulder.

"Want me to wait to take you back to the mainland?"

"No." Jonas glanced toward the small village. "If I don't find who I'm looking for, I'll get a hotel room."

"Things close down here pretty early even during the tourist season."

So he'd heard.

"Even if there is a room at one of the hotels or bed-and-breakfasts, you might not find anything open this late."

Then he'd be sleeping—more likely passing out—in the woods. Although these wet clothes would make for an interesting night, he'd probably survive.

He took a few steps toward the village before he remembered his manners, something he hadn't had much use of during the past couple of years. Turning back, he handed the man a tip. "Thanks for the ride and the warning, but I'll be all right."

"Suit yourself."

Jonas walked slowly down the pier to the drone of the boat motor behind him indicating the water taxi was heading out of the marina and back to the mainland. Soon even that sound dimmed. A few, thick drops spattered the ground, and the heavy clouds overhead threatened a nasty storm. Without a moon, the only light came from intermittent lampposts along the dock.

Gusts of wind whipped tree branches into a frenzy as he walked toward what appeared to be the central part of town. His shoes made barely a sound on the wet cobblestone. In the distance, a dog barked. He passed a blue-and-white restaurant, the Bayside Café, now closed and hit Main Street. Light from a place called Duffy's Pub spilled onto the sidewalk.

As he passed the bar, laughter and music emanated from inside, but he closed out the sound. Sometimes it was easier to forget that the world still housed polite, law-abiding people, going about living normal lives, raising normal families, working at normal jobs. Including him, once upon a long time ago.

That's when he'd met her. At a different bar with different music and different people. Had she changed? Most assuredly. It'd been years, not months. Years. He hesitated. No choice. The woods were sounding mighty cold and wet right about now.

Turning and crossing the street, he slowly climbed the steep hill several blocks off Main. With old, but well-kept single-family homes, this appeared to be the residential section of the tourist town. Instead of the Victorian mansions he'd halfway expected to see, these were average-size dwellings. He should've known she'd try to settle anonymously amidst the salt of the earth.

On hitting Oak Street, he turned and monitored the house numbers. Long ago, he'd memorized the address, wanting absolutely no paper trail for this place, and having studied the island map back at the ferry office, he knew he was close.

A few blocks later, he stopped in front of an ancient stone fence and glanced at the white Cape Cod with black shutters and a porch addition off the side. This modest home wasn't at all what he'd expected. The house was dark other than a stream of weak light glowing from the back. Her bedroom. She was still awake.

What did she look like? His dreams? His memories? Or had she shaken off the past and embraced change?

Time to find out.

Slowly, he trudged up the sidewalk, climbed the front steps and hesitated on reaching her porch as beads of sweat broke out on his brow. Quiet music sounded from inside, mixing with the damp night air as he leaned against a post and caught his breath.

This was a mistake. If she slammed the door in his face he couldn't blame her. After what he'd done, he unequivocally derserved it. Before he could turn away, the door burst open. A woman's figure, small but curvy stood in shadow, backlit by pale light. At first, he couldn't see her face, but then his eyes adjusted and her features cleared.

Oh, man. The air puffed out of his chest and his limbs went numb. When he'd first met her, she'd been only twenty-three to his thirty-two, going on fifty. Somehow, the years had made her even more beautiful than the day he'd spotted her in that hole-in-the-wall bar. She'd put on a little weight, which to his way of thinking only served to heighten the attractiveness of her curves. Her hair was longer and curlier, although the color was still that creamy blonde, promising the softness of down, the scent of heaven.

She said nothing, only stared at him as something akin to recognition dawned.

"Hello, Missy," he whispered.

She stepped back as if she'd seen a ghost, but then, he figured, she had. "Jonas," she whispered, putting a hand to her chest. "You're supposed to be dead."

"Better late than never," he mumbled as the adrenaline he'd been running on finally fizzled. His legs fell out from under him. He hit the wall, keeled over and collapsed onto the porch floor.

"Jonas? Jonas." Her hands touched his chest. Nice, soft hands. Hands that spread warmth all the way to his limbs. Hands he'd dreamed of more than he cared to remember. "Oh, my God, you're bleeding!"

Disoriented, he gazed into her eyes, eyes as startlingly

green as a new spring leaf, eyes that had once looked at him as if he were the only spot of clarity in her fuzzy crystal ball. "No doctors, Missy," he murmured, her face blurring in his vision. He could barely keep his eyes open. "Can't... no one...can find me."

Then his world turned black and silent.

CHAPTER TWO

WAS HE REAL OR SOME KIND of spirit?

Missy reached out to see if she could touch the man's arm and jerked back the instant her senses registered not only cold and wet, but a solid form. How could this be?

Maybe it wasn't really him.

Quickly, she took in everything about the man lying on her porch. His clothes, damp sweatshirt, faded jeans. Pushing aside the hood shadowing his face, she studied his features. Straight, hawklike nose. Intensely set brows, furrowed even now. Lashes, thick and black and long enough to set any woman's heart fluttering. So much so familiar, and yet enough that was different to make her wonder.

This man looked like a sleazy drug dealer. He probably hadn't taken a razor to his cheeks for weeks and his hair was not only long enough to curl it didn't look very clean. Jonas, always meticulous about his appearance, had kept his midnight-black hair military short and his face shaved as smooth as a baby's bottom. Then there was the hardness to this man's jawline that seemed all wrong. A cynical set to the mouth—

His mouth. That was it. The sight of this man's lips sealed it. How many times had she traced with the tip of her finger that dramatic upper arc? That full lower swell?

It *was* him. It was Jonas.

Missy snapped off the porch light and glanced around outside. Other than raindrops splattering her porch roof, all was quiet. There were no footsteps. No rustling of bushes. No shadows slinking near the trees. As far as she could tell no one had followed him.

Grabbing his wrist, she felt for a pulse. His skin was cold and clammy, but she located a thready pulse. He'd only lost consciousness. Glancing at his prone form, she barely held herself back from hauling off and kicking him good and hard. "I should let you bleed to death, you bastard."

The sight of his profile, haggard and worn, gave her pause. His skin was ashy and pale. "I'm going to hate myself for this." She grabbed his hands, dragged his dead-weight into her living room, snatched up his pack and shut the door. Then she put his knapsack off into the corner and bent over his still form.

His outer jacket had fallen open, displaying a patch of blood seeping through his sweatshirt. She pulled the fabric aside. A large padded bandage taped to his skin was soaked through with more blood. She eased off the bandage.

Oh, God. A bullet wound. Who would want to kill a man already dead to the world?

Although the shot appeared to have gone clear through Jonas's side, the wound was still bleeding. Grabbing a clean towel, Missy pressed it against the gaping holes, both front and back, but blood continued to flow. *No doctors.* What had he gotten himself into this time? Didn't matter. She couldn't do this on her own. The only problem was that gossip traveled on a little island the size of Mira-belle like rain down a gutter, but if she didn't act quickly—

Sarah? Too complicated.

Ron and Jan? Her neighbors, the Setterbergs, had become more like a mother and father since she'd moved to Mirabelle. They'd drop everything to help, but how could she explain Jonas? No. She couldn't handle disillusioning them. Not them.

Sean. He'd keep this quiet.

Grabbing the phone, she dialed his number only to hear a recorded message. "You've reached Dr. Griffin…"

At the end of the familiar greeting, she said, "Sean, it's Missy—"

The phone line crackled. "Missy?" He was obviously screening his calls. "You okay?"

"I'm fine, but I need your help. For someone at my house. Can you come right away?"

Sean lived only a few blocks down the street in a home very similar to Missy's. "What's the condition? I need to know what supplies to bring."

She hesitated. "A gunshot wound."

There was a long pause on the line. "What—"

"Please. He needs you right away."

"He? Missy—"

"I'll explain when you get here. Hurry."

She hung up, knelt back down and applied pressure to Jonas's wound. As she stared at his face, memories enveloped her. The helicopter wreckage, the charred black remains of a body, the wake, the funeral. It hadn't been a dream. It had been real. She'd relived every god-awful minute of it for years afterward. Jonas was supposed to be dead. Yet here he was on the floor, hurt but very much alive. It didn't make sense.

"How could you do this to me?" she whispered, emotion clogging her throat.

A brisk knock sounded on her front door. She peered through the curtain to find Sean standing on her steps, yanked open her door and ushered him inside.

Sean took one look at Jonas and, biting back the questions, flung off his raincoat and tossed it over a nearby chair. "Let's get him up somewhere, so I can work." A few moments later, after half carrying, half dragging Jonas's heavy body toward the back of her house, they had him lying atop her bed. "Let's get these wet clothes off him."

While Sean held up Jonas's limp frame, she tugged off his sweatshirt and shirt. "Get his pants off, too," Sean ordered as he went about cleaning the wound. "We need to get him warm."

Missy went to the waistband of Jonas's jeans and hesitated as her fingers touched the line of black hair trailing down his bare abdomen. Heat spread through her as she glanced at Jonas's toned upper body. He'd been lifting again, heavily, and his skin seemed darker than normal, as if he'd been in the sun.

"Missy!" Sean said, snapping her out of her appraisal. "We don't have any time to waste. This man's in shock. Get him warm. Quick."

She grabbed the waistband of Jonas's jeans and worked to undo the button, draw down the zipper and drag the damp fabric off his too-cool skin. Thank heavens his boxers remained relatively in place.

"Get every bit of wet fabric off him," Sean said. "Or it'll drain his heat."

"Everything?"

"Everything." Sean was pulling supplies out of his bag. "Now."

Missy did her best to avert her gaze as she tugged at

Jonas's boxers. The moment she cleared his ankles, she drew a heavy quilt over his lower body, but the image of his nakedness was already branded in her mind. No wonder no man had been able to measure up, in more ways than one, all these years.

Dammit. Stop it. He ruined your life once. Do not let him ruin it again.

Resolutely, she glanced at Sean. "What else can I do to help?"

A half hour later, Missy having assisted where needed, Sean had cleaned and stitched the entrance and exit wounds as well as two other cuts and had finally stopped the bleeding. While he'd been busy, they'd barely spoken other than requests for this and that.

He was wrapping Jonas's chest, when he said, "This guy's lucky the bullet went straight through his side, but he's got a broken rib. Various other cuts and contusions." He pointed at the slices on the side of his face, as if Jonas had been punched by a man wearing a ring, and the bruising on his arms and abdomen. "Someone really worked him over, but from the old scars it looks like he's used to it."

Missy well remembered the other bullet wound on Jonas's shoulder, but the three-inch scar on his right arm was something new.

"He'll need to be on antibiotics," Sean went on. "And he'll need this bandage changed at least—"

Jonas's hand shot out and grabbed Sean's wrist. His eyes fluttered open and he glared at Sean. "Who are you?"

"Jonas!" Missy hissed. "Let him go!"

Sean stared back at Jonas. "That's a damned strong grip for a half-dead man."

"Answer my question or lose a hand."

Sean's only sign of emotion was the slight flaring of his nostrils. Missy had never seen the calm, unflappable doctor this angry. She placed her hand on Jonas's. "Let him go right now, Jonas, or so help me God I will kick you out of my house!"

Without glancing at her, Jonas loosened his hold on Sean's wrist.

Sean slowly pulled away. "My name's Sean Griffin. I'm Mirabelle's only doctor."

Jonas threw an accusatory glance in her direction.

"I considered letting you bleed to death." She glared back at him. "But I wasn't sure how to dispose of the body."

Jonas turned back to Sean. "Tell anyone I'm here, and if I get the chance…I'll kill you."

"You hurt her—" Sean tilted his head toward Missy "—and I'll kill *you*."

Jonas's gaze flashed at Missy as he was assessing the connection between her and Sean. His eyes held the barest hint of betrayal before he quickly looked away. "Understood." Clearly in a lot of pain, he lowered his eyelids and seemed to focus on his breathing.

"Here." Sean poured a couple pills out of a bottle, reading Jonas better than most. "This'll help with the pain. Let you sleep."

"Don't need it," Jonas growled.

Sean sighed. "Fine." He set the medication on the bedside table.

Missy crossed her arms and frowned at Jonas. "You have a lot of explaining to do."

"It'll have to wait until morning."

"I want answers now."

He cocked his head toward Sean. "Then he needs to leave."

Sean shook his head. "I'm not going anywhere until I know Missy's safe. How do I know whoever shot you won't be showing up on her doorstep in the middle of the night?"

"Because I know how to cover my tracks. I'm not an idiot."

"You're idiot enough to almost get yourself killed."

Jonas made a quick move toward Sean, but clearly the pain knocked him flat on his back. "You don't know what you're talking about, Doc." Jonas gritted his teeth. "So why don't you just get the hell out of here?"

Glaring at Jonas, Missy quickly gathered the medical supplies and led Sean out of the bedroom and down the hall. "I'm sorry about all of this."

"It's not your fault." He stuffed everything she held back into his bag and glanced uncertainly into her eyes. "Maybe I should stay. I don't like the idea of leaving you here alone with that man."

That man. She almost laughed. "It's all right. He won't hurt me."

"You're sure?"

"Positive."

"Who is he, Missy?"

"An FBI agent. At least he used to be." That didn't answer the real gist of his question, but Missy didn't know where to begin.

Sean stared at her, as if trying to make sense out of the situation. From the moment he'd moved to the island last fall, Missy had felt a connection with him. Though he was guarded, rarely sharing anything of his past, she understood. She had secrets, too.

Most of the islanders speculated about a romantic relationship between her and Sean, but she'd never considered the two of them closing down Duffy's on more than one occasion as anything more than a good time, especially since he'd never officially asked her out or made any attempt to kiss her.

They were friends. Good friends, but still only friends. She could trust him, and she owed him the truth. At least part of it. "It's a long story," she whispered. "I need you to keep this between us."

"Missy?" He grabbed her hand and squeezed. "Who is he?"

She swallowed and looked into his eyes. "He's my husband."

JONAS STRUGGLED TO MAINTAIN consciousness, strained to hear the conversation taking place down the hall. Whispers. Quiet and intimate. Missy with another man. He didn't know why it should surprise him. As far as she knew, he was dead, and his death would've only given her a ticket to ride anything and anyone her freestyle heart desired.

Old familiar stirrings of jealousy reared up inside him and, at the sound of the front door closing and steps coming down the hall, he quickly tamped back the feelings. He couldn't spare the energy for jealousy. Not now. Not ever.

Slowly, Jonas retrieved his gun from the bedside table. He slipped it under the covers only seconds before Missy came back into the room, looking confused and unsettled. "Why—"

"Will your doctor tell anyone about me?" he interrupted, not at all up for the interrogation she was sure to be formulating.

"No."

"Who is he to you?" he murmured in spite of himself.

"None of your business."

"I need to—"

"You're dead, remember. You have no needs or rights when it comes to me!"

"Well, unless that divorce you were planning went through before my death, you're still my wife. And I'm still your husband."

"Husband? I haven't had a husband for more than four years. As a matter of fact, as absent as you were for most of our marriage, I'm not sure the term *husband* ever applied to you."

He closed his eyes and took several breaths in and out. "I just need to make sure your doctor can be trust—"

"He can be." She paced beside the bed. "Unlike some men I know Sean keeps his promises."

"Good for him," he murmured.

Suddenly tired to the bone, Jonas wrapped his fingers around the cold but oddly comforting grip of his gun. As he closed his eyes, the remembered sound of gunshots echoed through his mind. One. Two. Then, as if in slow motion, he once again saw Matthews taking a direct double hit to the chest and flying through the air.

Jonas remembered turning, his weapon drawn, and that's when he'd gotten hit in his side. He'd managed to fire off several shots. Before spinning out of the alley, he'd hazarded a quick glance at Matthews. His partner had been lying in a puddle on the ground, his head bent backward at an unnatural angle. Dead. This time for real.

Fatigue settled swiftly over Jonas. He was tired of the lie he'd been living these past years. Tired of trying to be someone he wasn't. Tired of…just plain-ass tired.

"Jonas?" Missy said.

Feigning sleep, although the reality wasn't far off, Jonas didn't answer. More so than hearing her, he sensed her stepping back, maintaining her distance.

"Jonas?" she said impatiently. "I want some answers."

He imagined her standing there with her arms crossed protectively in front of her, her chin tucked defensively. He let his breathing turn heavy and she hesitated. She wouldn't touch him. He knew it, was counting on it.

"Are you awake?" She waited a minute, maybe two, then he heard her rummaging through a dresser drawer. Suddenly, she spun around and flicked off the light. "Asshole," she muttered on her way out of the bedroom.

Yeah? Tell me something I don't already know.

"THE BIGGEST DEAL OF MY LIFE is coming together!" Delgado yelled. "You assured me nothing—nothing—would get in my way!"

"Don't worry." Pretending a calmness he sure as hell wasn't feeling, Mason Stein spoke into his cell phone while searching the frame of the couch. "You're still on."

"What about your renegade agent?"

The man who may have foiled Mason's plans to be on a tropical beach in about three weeks with a couple million in an offshore account? "We'll find him." He pulled out his switchblade. "Before he does any damage. You have my word."

"Your word doesn't mean shit to me," Delgado bit out. "You don't get your money until my deal goes through."

"That goes without saying, but it might not be a bad idea to move up your timetable."

"Impossible. This deal is done. It's going down in three

weeks, regardless. I want this taken care of before I get back to the States next week."

"I'm working on it."

"I get busted, my men get busted, or my inventory is confiscated and you're a dead man."

Click.

"Son of a bitch!" Mason shoved his phone in the holder at his waist and then slashed open a cushion with his knife. He gutted the couch. Nothing. The chair. More nothing.

Frustrated, he flung his knife across the room, and it stuck with a satisfying thud in a kitchen cabinet. He'd torn this damned apartment to pieces and had come up with zilch. No addresses or phone numbers. No laptop or memory devices. Not even a single cell phone record. The man took the concept of anonymity to an entirely new level. How were they going to find him when they had absolutely nothing to go on?

As Mason stood there his cell phone rang. He glanced at the display and answered. "Tell me you found him."

"Not a trace."

"Dammit!" he bit out. "I want—"

"Relax, Mason. With all that blood in the alley, he's dead or dying."

"Not good enough." Mason paced around the mess he'd created of furniture stuffing, hunks of broken dishes and fractured picture frames. An end table was the only piece of furniture still standing. "This is your fault. You told me he'd turn. You told me—"

"So I was wrong. Shoot me."

"I want the body." Mason struggled to keep his voice down. "Then I want it never found."

"What do you think I am, stupid? If he's identified, people are going to start asking questions. Did you tell Delgado?"

"I didn't have to tell him. His people did." Mason closed his eyes. "If I go down, I won't be going alone. Understand?"

"Oh, I understand. Do you?"

"What do you mean?"

"We're working outside the lines right now, remember? This is no-man's-land. So don't give me any more orders. Understand that?"

"Yeah," Mason muttered. *And when all this is over and done with, you're dead, no matter what.*

"Good. 'Cause we got bigger problems on our hands than you think."

"How could this get any worse?"

"He kept files."

"Of what?"

"All the evidence he turned over to you over the course of the last four years. He backed up everything on a memory stick."

Mason broke out in a cold sweat. "You gotta be shitting me."

"If we don't find him soon, he could turn everything over and we're dead anyway."

"Why didn't you grab his files while you had the chance?"

"Why didn't you kill him in the alley? If you had this wouldn't be a problem. Did you find anything at his apartment?"

"What do you think?" Mason barely held his temper in check. He hadn't really expected anything to be here, but every base had to be covered. "I have meetings tomorrow in D.C."

"I can handle things on this end."

"I'm telling you he's hiding with someone he knows. Someone he trusts. His father. His wife."

A loud laugh sounded over the line. "There is no one. Why do you think I suggested him for this assignment in the first place? No one in the world gives a rat's ass whether Jonas Abel lives or dies."

CHAPTER THREE

JONAS WOKE TO THE SOUND of a robin warbling loudly and quite happily outside the bedroom window. He glanced through the filmy pale green curtains and located the noisy little bastard perched on the branch of a massive elm tree. Lacking the energy to blow the damned thing to kingdom come, he squeezed his eyes shut and tried to ignore the sound.

What do you think you're doing?
Get up. Get it done. Do your job.

Sighing, he tried to sit and pain sizzled through him, knocking him back down. Damn, it felt as though his body had been first tenderized and then run through a man-size meat grinder. Apparently, that's what first getting jumped by four men, then shot, and then losing half the blood in his body did to a guy. He was in no shape to do anyone any damage.

Rolling over in the hopes of falling back asleep, he buried his head under a pillow. On his next breath the scent of something hauntingly familiar came to him. Something sultry and lush. Something that oddly enough had him feeling at once content and restless.

Screw sleep.

He cracked open his eyes to find a set of pale gold orbs

staring back at him. Cat eyes. Short-haired and black, but for a slit of white on its chest and a white sock on one rear paw, the cat sat serenely at the edge of the bed and studied him with curious disinterest. The animal had the muscular build of an outdoor cat and one of its ears was notched, most likely from a fight, ramping up the tough guy look.

"How did you get here?" he murmured.

From what he remembered, Missy had been frightened of cats since as a youngster she'd tried breaking up a couple of toms going at it. A nice long scar on the back of her left hand was all she had to show for her good-natured efforts. He, on the other hand, had absolutely no good reason for his dislike of cats.

The cat, taking his life in his own paws, crouched down and rubbed the side of his black head against Jonas's hand. Jonas's instinctive reaction was to flick the thing off the bed, but then the silkiness of the animal's fur against his calloused hands registered. It'd been a long time since anything that soft had touched his skin.

Unable to resist, Jonas turned his hand and scratched the underside of the cat's chin. The animal purred and pushed harder against Jonas's hand. The more he scratched the louder the purr. Before he knew it the damned thing was inching onto Jonas's chest looking for more.

"Oh, no you don't." He lifted the covers, unseating the animal and forcing it to the ground. Instead of being upset, the cat stretched languorously as if it'd been his plan all along to jump to the floor before walking slowly out of the room. "Cocky little shit."

Jonas chuckled, and another wave of pain moved through him. Considering taking something to make it through the day, he glanced at the bedside table. Clustered together were several small sample containers of prescription medicine and a large cup with a bendy straw that appeared to hold water. Apparently, the good doctor had left some halfway decent painkillers as well as an antibiotic and a sleep aid.

Awfully nice of Missy's *boyfriend.* And he was her boyfriend. Jonas was sure of that. The man had looked at her last night with a distinctly protective and proprietary air. How long had they been seeing one another? How much had she told the doctor about Jonas and their past?

Why should he care? He set the bottles down and knocked back a couple of ibuprofen. Movement sounded upstairs, followed closely by the running of a shower. Missy was not only awake, she was also most likely naked and wet. Now there was an image he didn't need running through his mind. Come to think of it, he was buck naked himself under the covers. How had that happened?

Missy. He had a vague recollection of her hands brushing his skin, her fingers on his stomach as she worked the zipper on his jeans. *Think of something else, you idiot.* The last thing he needed in his sorry state was a hard-on.

After prepping himself with a slow, measured breath he threw back the green leaf-printed comforter—knowing Missy, it was probably organic cotton—then gingerly rolled onto his good side and slowly pushed himself to a sitting position. Damn, he felt weak. As he waited for the rush of light-headedness to pass, he located his pack on the floor by the door, looking as though it'd been left unopened. Good. That was good.

Still waiting for equilibrium, he glanced around the room. The woodwork was enameled white, but the rich, milk chocolate-brown on the walls seemed to curiously vary in shade from one side to the next. Knowing Missy, and her tendency toward impulsiveness, she'd changed her mind while in the middle of painting.

The furniture was a mishmash of wicker, metal and some kind of natural hardwood. A big, leafy plant hung from the ceiling near the window, and a couple smaller pots sat on the dresser and bedside tables. A collage of different shaped and sized photos covered the wall above the headboard of the bed.

He might've thought it a guest bedroom but for the jewelry lying atop the long dresser. Beads, crystals, metal pendants or Chinese coins. It was exactly the kind of stuff Missy would wear—

He'd slept in Missy's room. In her bed. No wonder the scent on the pillow had felt so familiar. That's when he noticed something hanging over the arm of the nearby wicker chair next to his jeans. He picked up the pale yellow scrap of fabric and held it out. A nightgown. Flimsy. Lacy. Sexy as hell, especially if he imagined Missy in it with her long curls, her beautiful shoulders, her breasts—

Full-blown hard-on. He swallowed and hung his head. What a loser. After all these years, after the way she'd turned on him and broken his heart, how could he still want her?

The gown felt soft and slippery in his hand. Had she ever worn it for the doctor? Was she sleeping with him?

That's none of your damned business. She doesn't want your sorry old ass. She made that more than clear, remember? Besides, you've got work to do, so get to it so you can get off this hunk of rock floating in the middle of nowhere.

He grabbed his jeans, dug out the memory stick attached to a lanyard he'd hidden in a secret pocket in the thick waistband and hung it around his neck. After releasing a deep breath, he stood, tested his balance, then rummaged through his pack, verifying that his laptop had not been compromised.

After pulling on some clothes and tucking his gun inside the waistband of his sweats, he made his way slowly down the hall and into the main living area of the house. The space felt airy and open without any barriers between the kitchen and living room, living room and all-season porch.

Footsteps sounded behind him and, instantly on alert, he spun around. Pain shot up his side at the sudden twisting and he cringed.

Missy was coming down the stairs. "We have to talk." She barely glanced at him as she moved past to put a tea-kettle on the stove.

The pain, mostly, subsided. "I'm not sure we have any-thing to say to one another."

"Well, I have plenty to say to you, but first I want some answers." She scooped some loose tea leaves into a metal mesh container and then focused on him. "Why aren't you dead?"

Oh, yeah, that.

Jonas carefully eased himself onto one of the bar stools at her kitchen counter and studied her. Apparently having grabbed what she'd needed for today before she'd left him last night, she'd dressed simply, in a pair of straight-legged jeans and a long, loose, short-sleeved brown sweater. With naturally clear skin, she'd never needed much makeup. Her hair hung in damp curls. The only jewelry she wore was a necklace, a couple of hefty faceted quartz crystals strung on a strip of woven leather.

But it was the way she carried herself that set her apart. He couldn't believe he hadn't noticed it the first time he'd met her, the way she held herself, so straight and confidently. The regal set of her chin, angled slightly downward as if she were looking down upon the masses. Her hands. Long, royal-looking fingers and bones so fine she looked as if he could break her in half.

There were changes, too. Not a lot, not enough that most people would notice, but noticing things was part of his job. Her easy way of smiling seemed to have been replaced by a touch of seriousness about her mouth. There was more depth to her eyes, a more sober line to her brow. Was it possible she'd matured inside as well as out? He wasn't holding his breath.

"I'm not dead because there was no helicopter crash," he finally answered. "It was staged."

"Brent Matthews? The other agent in the helicopter with you?"

"No one died, Missy."

"There were two bodies," she said as if she couldn't quite wrap her mind around this twist in the past. "I saw them. I saw...your body."

If he didn't know better, he'd have said a shadow of something damned close to sadness momentarily passed over her features. "John Does from the morgue." He shook his head. "They put the bodies in the shell of the chopper before they blew it up."

"Why?"

"Because they didn't expect me to live through the undercover assignment I'd accepted." He almost hadn't. "On top of that, they knew it would be long-term and they wanted absolutely no contact with family or friends. I received a totally new identity, and I've been on that same case ever since."

"So you're still with the FBI. How long were you under-cover?"

"It took us a couple years to infiltrate the group. Since then, it's been another two years." He sighed. "Plus."

"You've been living someone else's life for four years?"

"It's my job."

"Your job." Clearly disgusted, she shook her head. "You're the same as you've always been, aren't you? The job is still the only thing that matters in your life."

How often had she thrown that accusation in his face? Well, it may not have been as true all those years ago, but it sure as hell was true now. After all that time undercover, living as he had surrounded by lawless, disrespectful thugs, getting hardened to seeing things he hadn't wanted to see, there were days even he didn't recognize the man he'd become.

"Why'd you agree to do it?"

"I think the more appropriate question is why not?" After watching his father stand ineffectively by while his mother slowly died, Jonas had wanted nothing to do with the dead-beat. He'd never had any siblings, no relatives at all, really. At the time Stein had come to him with the risky undercover opportunity, Missy had been his only family. When she turned her back on him, he had nothing left in the world.

"Why not?" She glared at him. "Because you had a wife and a father. A life."

"Did I?" he bit out. If he hadn't felt so weak, he would've stood and paced the floor of her kitchen. As it was, all he could do was sit there. "You filed for a divorce, Missy. Remember that part of the equation?"

The morning she told him she'd seen an attorney, he'd felt as if he'd been hit dead on by a train. Bam! Life gone.

Rejected. Start over. That's exactly what he'd deserved for letting himself get carried ass-over-teakettle away by an immature young woman. He'd thought himself in love, and he'd found out the hard way there was no such thing.

Love. Right.

If Jonas had known the truth about her age, about who Missy really was when he'd first met her, he never would've married her, let alone had sex with her in the back of his SUV the first night they'd met. Hell, there had to be any number of women in the world who shared her name. Who would've ever guessed she was *the* Melissa Camden? He was still pissed she hadn't told him the truth about her background until a few days before their wedding.

He'd tried, he really had, to look beyond it, to see Missy for who she was and not what her family had made her, but his pride had been hurt too much to recover. He'd soon had to face the fact that he could never have supported her in a lifestyle in any way, shape or form close to what she'd been used to. From the beginning, the deck had been stacked against them.

"The way I see it," he said, unable to keep the bitterness from his voice, "my death just made things easier for you." Not to mention that a small, stupid part of him had inexplicably reasoned that she'd still be his wife.

"Easier?" She laughed, but the sound was laced with what sounded a lot like desperation. "How was that supposed to make it easier? For me?"

"Bang. I was out of your life. No attorneys. No messy division of assets. One little funeral and it was over." He shrugged. "I'll bet you didn't even cry."

She fell silent. Then that damned cat jumped onto the counter and rubbed against her. She snuggled the animal to her chest, scratched its neck and glanced back at him. "No, you're right. I never cried. Not one single tear. Satisfied?"

No, he wasn't even close to being satisfied with what had happened between him and Missy, but he'd accepted the fact long ago that he'd made a rash decision in marrying her. Everyone knew a man didn't need to care deeply about a woman to be elementally and viscerally attracted to her. What a lot of people didn't realize was that some women— women like Missy—could be the same way.

Apparently, if the quick rise and fall of her chest were any indication, she hadn't changed. As if she remembered the heat that had unfailingly risen between them, the long hours spent simply pleasing each other, her gaze caught with his and held.

He'd never known a more passionate, uninhibited woman than Missy. All he'd ever had to do was touch her face and she'd melted in his hand. Caress her breast and she'd arch to meet him. Touch his tongue to hers and she'd do anything he'd ask. What he wouldn't give to find out if he still held that kind of power over her. All it would take was one touch to find out. Just one.

The teakettle whistled in the heavy silence and she spun around. *Damn.* After putting down the cat, she flipped off the burner and poured steaming hot water into a metal travel mug. "Your dad was at your funeral," she said softly, dipping the mesh tea holder into the hot water.

When the cat walked toward Jonas, clearly looking for more affection, he quickly stood and searched through her kitchen cabinets for something to eat. All those years ago, he'd been sorely tempted to go to his own funeral, but life as he'd known it was over. A clean break had been for the best.

"He was pretty broken up," she whispered, turning.

"Yeah. Whatever." Jonas couldn't keep the bitterness from his voice.

He'd been only twelve when he'd lost all respect for his father. The man had lost one job after another and finally their home. He hadn't even been able to cover the medical bills that had accumulated as doctors treated Jonas's mother's heart condition. Eventually, they'd lost her, too. How could a man call himself a man if he couldn't provide for his family?

Jonas pulled a cereal box out of the cupboard and glanced at it. Organic sticks and twigs. "You got any coffee?"

"What do you think?"

"Still on that health kick, huh?"

"Jonas?" She put her hands on the counter and stared at him. "What are you doing here?"

That was the toughest question of all. He turned away, opened the refrigerator and held out a carton of soymilk, unflavored to boot. "This all you have?"

"Why here?"

The damned cat sat in the middle of the kitchen floor staring at him as if he, too, waited for an answer.

"I've always wanted an island vacation." He shrugged, taking out a bowl. "Figured—"

"Don't mess with me." She grabbed his arm and, as he turned toward her, just as quickly let go.

She was so close he could smell the scent of something spicy coming off her hair, see the dark green flecks in her pupils, and nearly feel the suppleness of her pink lips. If he kissed her, would he be able to remind her how much she'd once wanted him and no other man?

Lot of good it would do.

"Why Mirabelle?" she asked. "Why now?"

The cat proceeded to weave itself between his legs. Damned thing didn't have an ounce of sense. It was on the tip of his tongue to ask Missy how she'd ended up with the animal, but the question would imply an interest in her life and he couldn't afford to open that door. He was here to heal and think. That was all. He backed away and the cat, as if it'd had enough of him, crossed the room and hopped outside through a kitty door. Jonas might as well do the same thing and get this over with.

"I've been in Chicago undercover for the last four years," he said. "We were only a couple of weeks from making a huge bust when something went wrong. I haven't figured it out yet, but somehow my cover was blown and all hell broke loose. They jumped me in an alley. It all happened so fast I'm not even sure who they were. One thing led to another and somehow I got shot. I need time to put the pieces together."

"Why here? Why me?"

"I needed a place to hide. Somewhere I wouldn't be found. And no one knows where you are. You did a damned good job of getting lost."

Shortly after he'd died, she'd changed her name several times and her attorneys had made the paper trail extremely difficult to follow. She didn't want her family to find her, and Jonas understood. While they'd been together, Missy had shared in great depth her family issues, mostly her problems with her overly controlling father. His own father might be a loser, but Missy's was an outright asshole.

Jonas would never forget the shot to his pride when her dad took him aside on their wedding day. "She met you in a bar, Abel," he'd said. "You might as well give it up right now. If your father's track record is any indication, you will never be able to provide the lifestyle my daughter deserves."

While it'd pissed Jonas off to no end that Missy's father had run a background check on Jonas, the man had called it all right. Jonas had worked his ass off. No matter what he did or didn't do, it was never enough. He would never earn her father's respect. In the end, he'd only ended up regretting putting a bigger wedge between Missy and her family. It was another reason why his death had seemed like the right thing to do. With him out of the way, he'd hoped she might reconcile with her family. So much for that.

"Obviously, I didn't get lost enough," Missy said, bringing his thoughts back to the present. "*You* found me."

Only because he'd kept track of her since day one, following her name changes and moves from town to town for the first couple of years. She'd done a helluva job covering her tracks, and just when her trail had finally gone cold to the rest of the world, she'd upped and moved once more for good measure, settling on Mirabelle. What had surprised him more than anything was that she'd settled on using Missy, the nickname he'd given her within the first few weeks of meeting.

"How?" she asked. "How did you find me?"

He shrugged again.

"You've been following me all this time."

"Following? Don't flatter yourself."

"What would you call it, then?"

"Morbid curiosity?" Or the need to make sure she was at least at peace, if not happy, that he hadn't completely ruined her life.

"I don't buy it," she said. "You could hide anywhere."

Time to suck it up. "Okay. The truth." As hard as it was, he held her gaze. "I know it's going to sound crazy, but you're the only person I can trust." He might not be able to trust her with his heart, but with his life? She could no sooner turn him in than gnaw on a T-bone. "You're all I got, Missy."

CHAPTER FOUR

THE ONLY PERSON HE COULD TRUST?

To anyone who didn't know Jonas that might've sounded like quite the stretch, but he'd always been a loner. And she'd always been a sucker for lost causes, especially where Jonas was concerned.

Oh, for God's sake, the man broke your heart. Twice. First by proving over and over again he'd preferred his job to her and then again when he'd faked his death.

Her memories tracked to the deep despair and loneliness that had set in not long after they'd returned from their honeymoon. One day Missy and Jonas were lying together in each other's arms making plans for the future, and the next she was lying alone, night after night, weekend after weekend while some invisible demon pushed Jonas in his job. Trying to talk about it had only seemed to push him farther away.

Then, just when she'd begun contemplating divorce, she'd gotten pregnant. Hope had bloomed inside her. A child is what they'd needed to bind them more closely together, but she'd held off telling Jonas. What if things didn't change? What if he remained lost in his job?

Maybe somewhere deep inside she'd known something was wrong with the pregnancy. She'd miscarried at ten weeks. In the blink of an eye, it was all over. She'd curled up in that hospital bed alone, unable to reach Jonas, cramping, bleeding, losing not only their baby, but all hope for their marriage. She'd been completely unprepared for the pain that had set in after she'd thought Jonas had died.

"Missy," he said, pulling her back to her kitchen, to this reality that seemed so unreal. "I need—"

"No," she said. "You can't stay here. I can't—"

"Missy—"

"There must be another agent. What about Brent Matthews?"

"Dead. This time for real." Jonas paused, swallowed. "They nailed him in the alley. He took two bullets directly in the chest before the shooter turned on me."

She felt herself wavering. Brent had seemed like a good man. Years ago, just after she'd married Jonas, she'd met him once or twice at various Bureau functions along with a few other agents and their wives and girlfriends. She'd always wondered whether or not getting a chance to connect with those other women would have helped her weather the—mostly—downs of Jonas's job.

She gave a brisk shake of her head. "You must have someone else—"

"Some things aren't adding up. Someone at the Bureau might be involved, and I don't know who I can trust."

"What kind of assignment were you on?"

"Undercover in a Colombian drug-trafficking ring."

Drugs. Something about that raised the fine hair on the back of her neck. *Oh, God.* "Does my father know you're alive?"

Missy's father, Arthur Camden, had been a United States senator, ultraconservative and extremely powerful, for as long as anyone could remember. Although he was the chairman of the Senate Judiciary Committee, which had FBI oversight, he had a reputation for putting his fingers in any governmental pie that struck his fancy. He'd been as controlling and manipulative at home with his family as he was on Capitol Hill.

"No," Jonas answered. "The Judiciary Committee wasn't getting briefed on the status of our mission."

"Are you sure? The war against drugs was one of his pet projects for years."

"This was a covert op," Jonas said. "These days Congress is concerning itself more with national security. You know damned well your father is at the front of that line."

He was probably right, but Missy had a bad feeling about this whole deal. "You have to leave."

"Why?" He studied her with a gaze that left no stone unturned, promised to ferret out every secret.

Damned FBI agents. "Because I said so."

He shook his head. "It's good to know some things never change. You're still as irrational as ever."

She spun toward him. "I'm irrational? Just because I follow my instincts rather than analyze every decision?"

"Call it whatever you want. Impulsive. Hasty. Spontaneous. All the same to me."

"There's nothing wrong with being spontaneous, but you wouldn't know anything about that, would you?" The man wouldn't know how to relax and have fun if he was sitting on a sandy beach and someone shoved an umbrella drink in his hand.

"And some people use spontaneity as an excuse." He narrowed his eyes. "Covers up a helluva lot of irresponsibility."

"I am not now, never have been, irresponsible. No matter what you think." Immature once upon a time, yes. Never, ever irresponsible.

"Well it certainly helps having some money in a trust fund backing your play, doesn't it?"

She straightened her shoulders. "For your information, I support myself from the proceeds from my own gift shop. For years, the only substantial money going out of my trust fund has been for donations."

Oddly enough the biggest drain on her resources had been Mirabelle itself. The island had been sucking air a couple years back and a lot of businesses had been about to go under. Marty Rousseau had proposed building a golf course and pool and had promised to pay for part of it himself. When no other investors could be found, Missy had stepped in and directed her trust fund advisors to secretly buy the rest of the municipal bonds necessary to fund the projects. But she sure wasn't going to explain that to Jonas.

He narrowed his eyes at her. "You support yourself entirely off income from your gift store?"

"Not entirely." She backtracked. "I could if I focused purely on sales, but my gift shop is about something other than profit."

"So you do tap the trust fund for yourself?"

"Only small amounts for monthly living expenses."

"Figures."

As if they hadn't spent more than a few days separated, the old arguments that had torn them apart resurfaced. They stood, glaring at each other. Neither of them admitting any wrongdoing. Both of them stubborn in their righteousness. How could she have ever believed this man was the one true love of her life?

But she had. Jonas had steadied her world after she'd dropped out of college and spent years running from the only life she'd known as the privileged daughter of wealthy, connected, and ultraconservative parents. He'd treated her like a normal, everyday person.

He'd helped her grow, mature, and reaffirmed for her what she'd always known in her heart. That there was so much more to life than the one her father had wanted her to live. She'd been happy for the first time. She'd been ashamed to tell him her background, afraid it would change things between them. Maybe it had. It wasn't long after he'd found out the truth about her family that his work had taken hold of him and she couldn't seem to shake him loose.

"Still sending thousands of dollars off to rescue turtles or baby seals or dalmatians?" he asked with disdain.

She straightened her shoulders, preparing to argue, but he was right. While they'd been married, she'd liberally tapped into her account for any and every cause. If someone asked, she cut a check. "I'm more careful with donations these days."

"Buy any houses lately?"

That was a low blow. "Maybe if you'd been around more," she ground out, "I wouldn't have had to buy a house on my own." She'd thought making a cozier home for them would make him want to be there more often. Instead, she'd been left behind getting bored in their house rather than in their apartment.

No, not bored. Lonely. She'd missed him terribly. Missed his energy, his dark sense of humor, his deep, hearty laugh. She'd missed the way her body felt when he was near, the way he'd listened to her as if she was the only person that mattered in his world. Before Jonas, she'd lived such a sheltered life in so many ways. He'd always encouraged her to find herself, to find things she enjoyed doing and creating. He'd helped her begin to see that Melissa Camden had a Missy Charms locked inside.

Then he died. That's when the real loneliness set in. Her family, the people she should've been able to lean on, had only made things worse.

She glanced away from Jonas, the memories almost overwhelming. Her anger lost its fire. "My family came to your funeral. Even Charlie."

Charlie Steele was the man Missy's parents had tried to steer her toward most of her life. He was sweet and pleasant enough, but cut from the same cloth as his parents, her parents and her siblings. "The dirt had barely settled on your grave before my father turned to me and said…" She paused, unable to force out the words.

Jonas's glare softened ever so slightly.

She'd never forget the superior look in her father's eyes that day, or the way the words had felt branded into her brain. "'You've had your fun, Melissa,' he said. 'Now come home. Consider yourself fortunate you're through with the man without losing a penny. Charles has already agreed to take you back. All will be as it should be.'"

Jonas clenched his jaw.

"I'm not ready for him to find me, Jonas. Not now. Probably not ever."

Knowing she could never go back with her family, she'd packed her bags and floundered on her own for months, desperately trying to break free from her family, her name. Her father had hired detectives who always seemed to find her. The media would track down his men tracking her down. Very quickly, she'd gotten good at hiding her trail.

She'd transferred her trust fund to a management firm that had no dealings with the rest of the Camden clan. The company was given strict instructions to never disclose any information on her whereabouts to anyone. When the decision to start her own family and adopt had settled in her heart, she'd gotten serious about getting lost and finding a place to raise children. She'd found exactly what she was looking for on Mirabelle—a home, people she cared about and who cared about her.

Another blink of an eye and all that could change, too.

"I understand, Missy. I do." Jonas ran a hand through his long hair. "Dammit, all I'm asking for is a few days. At most a couple weeks."

"Weeks? Living here? Are you out of your mind?"

"Missy—"

"I'll give you one day and one day only to rest up from that gunshot wound."

"Mighty gracious of you."

"The first ferry leaves Mirabelle at seven in the morning." She wrapped her arms around herself, hoping to contain her emotions. "Tomorrow. I want you on that boat."

"Sorry to disappoint, Miss, but I'm not going anywhere." He sat at the counter with a carton of soymilk and a box of cereal. "Not yet, anyway."

"You can't stay here. I mean it, Jonas."

"I can. I will."

"This is a small island. I know everyone and everyone knows me—"

"Lot of friends here, then?"

"Yes—"

"They'd do anything to protect you? Like your doctor?"

"One call and our police chief, Garrett—"

"What, Missy? He'll arrest me? Throw me in jail? Kick me off the island? For what? I show him my badge and explain that I'm your husband. It's only a matter of time before the fact that you're a Camden comes out, and everyone on this island knows you for the liar you are."

She stepped back, feeling as shocked as if he'd slapped her face. It wasn't just that her father was a well-known senator. The name Camden fell right in line with several other historically famous, not to mention extremely wealthy, American last names. Missy's great-great-grandfather had not only been an inventor and engineer, he'd also been one of America's early entrepreneurs, making millions while this country's economy boomed.

"I've never lied to anyone on Mirabelle," she said. "Or to you. Never."

"A lie of omission is still a lie. I'll bet my last dollar you've *omitted* telling everyone on this island who you are and where you come from. Right, Missy *Charms?* What will all the simple folk of Mirabelle think of you after they find out your real last name is Camden?"

In truth, she hadn't purposefully lied to anyone. She'd stopped using her father's name back in college. Sick of year after year of having people act differently around her as soon as they found out who she was, she'd decided to be someone else.

She never told anyone her real last name. Not anymore. These days people saw Missy the way she wanted to be seen. She hadn't even told Jonas until a few days before their wedding. He'd told her it didn't matter, but a part of her had always wondered if he'd ever truly forgiven her. He didn't understand. Not really.

"When all your friends here find out you grew up in a

mansion out east," he went on. "Spent your summers flitting between your family compounds on Long Island and Los Angeles and the villa in the south of France. How many folks here on Mirabelle do you think have skied the Swiss Alps? Gone to an Ivy League university? Got driven around by chauffeurs most of their childhood?"

Embarrassed, Missy looked away. She'd never felt a part of the Camden clan. It wasn't just about her father, either. As a vegetarian, tree-hugging hippie she'd never fit with any of them. While her sister and two brothers had excelled in competitive sports, Missy had preferred yoga. They consumed, she recycled. They voted right-wing, she left. They spent on designers, she donated to nonprofits.

"What would Mirabelle folks think, Missy, of your hundred million dollar trust fund?"

There was no telling for sure. A few would think nothing of it. Others would want—expect—things from her. Still others would act strangely, awkwardly around her. All she wanted was anonymity. "You wouldn't do that to me."

"Wouldn't I?"

"Just for some time to figure out what went wrong with your stupid assignment?"

"You got it."

"There it is. Still alive and kicking," she said bitterly. "That blind and unwavering commitment to the job." In the end, she'd been bested by the Bureau.

"You've never been more right." He cocked his head at her. "Nothing's changed. I *was* the job. I still *am* the job. So until I figure out what went wrong on my *job,* I'm not leaving here."

As they faced each other off, his gaze momentarily landed on her necklace. Last night, after he'd first fallen asleep in her bed, she'd flashed on the image of him naked and her skin had flushed with heat. Feeling the need for a shield, she'd snatched up the crystals along with a change of clothing.

"Those look suspiciously like Arabic letters." He reached out and examined the pendant. "The Ayat al-Kursi," he whispered. "Verse of the throne." Jonas could not only read Arabic, he could speak a couple different dialects, along with German and Spanish. "What do you need protection from?" he murmured.

"Not what," she said softly. "Who."

Looking surprisingly offended, he dropped the crystals as if they'd singed his skin. "Still have those divorce papers?"

"Oddly enough," she said, "I kept them." She'd needed a reminder that a divorce is what she'd intended even before he died.

"Give me two, three weeks tops to heal and figure out who tried to kill me and why." Looking entirely spent, he started back toward her bedroom. "Then I'll sign your damned divorce papers and get the hell out of your life. This time for good."

CHAPTER FIVE

"ARE THE T-SHIRTS ON THIS RACK discounted, too?"

A couple of hours after Missy's confrontation with Jonas, she stood in the middle of her gift shop, looking steadily into a tourist's sunburned face. For the life of her, she couldn't seem to focus on the words coming out of that lipsticked mouth. All she'd been able to think about was the fact that her husband was alive.

Four years, five months, one week and three days.

That's how long it had been since Jonas had—supposedly—died. If necessary, she could calculate the passage of time down to the minute. The FBI had come to her house to tell her the helicopter had crashed at exactly 1:58 in the afternoon. He'd died on impact, they'd said. There was nothing anyone could've done. Still, she'd insisted on seeing his body and had fallen apart at the sight of what she'd believed were his charred remains.

Now where was that son of a bitch of a dead husband? Hanging out in her home, doing God only knows what. Simply imagining him in her private space, in the house she'd worked so hard to turn into a relaxed and comfortable haven, threw off her balance. She glanced around at the other tourist or two moseying around her shop and took a deep breath, hoping to clear her head.

"T-shirts?" the woman in front of her said, not a little irritated. "On sale?"

"I'm sorry. Just the rack in the corner is thirty percent off."

The woman shook her head and rolled her eyes. "Then you should be more specific with your signage."

Normally, Missy would've ignored the comment, but this morning was nowhere near normal. "Don't like it?" she said, raising her eyebrows. "You can leave."

The unrepentant comment had no sooner left her mouth, than she recognized it as having come from the old Missy. The spoiled, immature, reckless and rash Melissa Camden. The young woman who had unapologetically married Jonas less than three months after meeting him. The woman who had pouted—she had to be honest, at least with herself—when Jonas had had to work late or leave town for an assignment.

"Well, I never!" The woman roughly hung the shirt back on the rack and huffed out of the shop.

Missy glanced around. *One down. Two more to go.*

Apparently, Jonas barging back into her life had somehow thrown Missy back in time, as if she'd lost the past four plus years of growing and maturing. She'd been only twenty-three when she'd met him and an immature twenty-three at that. But she'd known what she'd wanted back then. Him.

She'd been doing tarot readings, for fun, at the bar she was working at in Quantico, Virginia. To this day, she had no clue what had drawn her to that town, but back then she wasn't questioning much. She'd broken free of her father and the last thing she'd wanted was structure or rules. She'd been letting her instincts and intuition drive her on the way to discovering this world.

What had driven her on the night she'd met Jonas had

been her body. She'd wanted him, and she was going to have him. They'd made love in the back of his SUV, and from that moment on she'd believed she was supposed to spend the rest of her life with him.

How could Fate have been so wrong?

Missy pressed the inside of her left arm against her side, putting close to heart the chakra symbols she'd had tattooed there not long after Jonas had supposedly died. *Steady, Missy. Remember who you are. Remember who you've become.*

Maybe Jonas dying had been the best thing that had ever happened to her. She'd been forced to find herself apart from who she was with him. Being on Mirabelle had helped her become Missy Charms, the responsible, respectful, albeit a bit flighty, woman who ran her own small business.

She paid her bills, mostly by the due dates, and she'd employed the same student for several summers in a row, helping the young woman, Gaia, make her way debt-free through college. Whimsy might not yet be breaking even, but she had the luxury of not having to worry about making a buck.

Not the typical, north woods, painted-fish-mailbox kind of gift shop, Missy inventoried, among other things, candles and incense burners, tarot cards and wind chimes, Buddha statues and water fountains, unique books and greeting cards made from recycled materials, clothing made from organic fabric and handmade jewelry, some of which Missy made herself.

In a place like Los Angeles, her wares would've likely flown off the shelves, but the Mirabelle residents had all thought she was crazy. Maybe she was. Maybe her gift shop never would break even. The important part was that all of her inventory came from either small U.S. businesses, more often than not owned by women trying to eke out a living, or foreign fair trade markets. There were more important things on her agenda than turning a profit.

Missy glanced around her shop and tried to shake off all her misgivings. Stretching out her neck to relax, she walked to the main desk, lit a stick of pine-scented incense and stuck it in a holder on the counter. The clean scent might go a long way in clearing her head and helping her dispel the negative energy she seemed to be carrying around with her since confronting Jonas that morning.

Slim sauntered into the store from the back room and Missy picked him up. "You're even better than incense," she whispered.

Since rescuing him as a tiny mewling kitten, the silky softness of Slim's thick coat never ceased to take her to a calm, comfortable place. Of course, Missy spoiled him, but how could she not? He followed her everywhere, often walking with her down to the shop to hang for a few hours. Whenever he got bored, he'd simply climb out into the alley through his little door and find his own way home.

"Psst, Missy." The quiet voice came from behind her.

She spun around to find Ron Setterberg, her neighbor and surrogate father as well as owner of the equipment rental shop a couple blocks away, peeking out of her back room. The cat had probably followed Ron here.

"Just thought I'd stop by and visit for a sec." He usually visited once a day, either at her shop, or after work in the early evenings at home. "Jan has the day off, so I'm heading to the house to have lunch with her."

Ron and his wife, Jan, the manager of the Mirabelle Island Inn, never had any children of their own, so they had pretty much adopted Missy since she'd moved to Mirabelle. Aside from Ron helping with repair work, he and Jan also invited Missy to their home for the occasional Sunday brunch and always for holiday meals.

"You got a sec?" Ron asked.

"Sure. Gaia?" Missy signaled to her helper. "You got things covered?"

"No problem."

Holding Slim in her arms, Missy followed Ron into the back room, stepping over boxes of inventory piled on the floor. She could never resist ordering more than she needed of almost everything. Putting food on needy tables took precedence over her storage issues. "What's up?"

He glanced around and his gaze landed on the storage shelves he'd purchased for her months ago still sitting unassembled in their original boxes. "You know it wouldn't take me long to put those together. I could have this storage room organized in a day." He'd been offering his assistance off and on ever since Missy had first started renting this retail space from him and Jan.

"Getting organized implies the possibility of staying organized." Missy grinned. "We both know there's not much likelihood of that happening." All she really cared about was making sure the cat door was free and clear so that Slim could get in and out whenever he liked.

"One of these days the bug's going to bite you," he said, slipping between a couple tall stands of boxes. "I repaired that display case for you and set it back here by the door." He showed her how to work the key to open the lock.

"Thanks, this'll be great for some of the more expensive jewelry," she said. "How you feeling today?" He looked a little flushed.

"Blood pressure's still acting up a bit. Sean's got me on

a new medication, so we'll see." He studied her face. "What's your excuse? You don't look so hot this morning."

"Gee, thanks."

"You know what I mean." He put his arm around her shoulder and squeezed. "Been eating right? Personally, I think you could use a nice juicy Delores burger."

Ron never could quite accept Missy being a vegetarian. He was always wanting her to try one of Delores Kowalski's cheeseburgers at the Bayside Café by the marina.

"I'm fine, Ron. Just didn't sleep well last night."

How was she going to hide Jonas's presence from him and Jan? More important, what would the couple say if she told them the truth about herself? What would all the islanders do, say, think if they found out she was a Camden?

If Jonas had never forgiven her for keeping her Camden heritage from him, it was entirely possible Ron and Jan wouldn't forgive her, either. How could they possibly understand where she'd come from, let alone her reasons for hiding from her past? At the very least, they might start treating her differently.

She recalled too many instances where people changed how they related to her simply because of her last name and the money behind it. On campus, teachers at college either expected too much from her or didn't expect enough. Students were either jealous or bent over backward wanting to be her friend. Out shopping with her mother and sister, some of the most dreadful experiences of her life, store clerks would see them coming and turn their backs on the other clients just to please the Camdens. As long as Missy had waved the Camden flag, she'd no hope for honesty.

She hugged Slim tighter, nuzzled her nose in his neck. No, she couldn't tell Ron and Jan. She couldn't risk losing the relationship she had with them.

"Hey," she said, putting aside all the negative thoughts as she set Slim down. "I've got something for you." He'd been complaining of various ailments, so Missy had put together a box of homeopathic remedies, teas and vitamin supplements. "Here you go." She held it out to him.

"What's this?"

"Stuff to help you feel better." She smiled. "It can't hurt, anyway."

"Well then, you'd better put together a care package for Jan, too." He patted her cheek. "Neither one of us is getting any younger." He'd be celebrating his sixty-fifth birthday soon with a backyard barbecue, but Missy refused to think about the possibility of them retiring and moving south.

"Hey, now that I think about it, I repaired your hair dryer," he said, heading toward the door. "I'll bring it on by the house sometime tonight."

"No, that's okay," she said, not ready yet to explain Jonas. "I'll come by and get it." She'd told Jonas in no uncertain terms that he was not to leave her house, but she wasn't going to be able to keep him secret for long.

Missy's cell phone rang. She'd been expecting a call from a supplier with whom she'd been playing telephone tag, so she quickly glanced at the display. The adoption agency. What was going to happen when they found out about Jonas?

Ron noticed the name glowing on her phone. "That Barbara? Aren't you going to answer it?"

Missy had been sharing her adoption trials and tribulations with Ron and Jan since she'd moved to Mirabelle. She couldn't close him off now.

"Well, go on," he said. "She might have good news."

Missy answered the call. "Hi, Barbara. What's up?"

"You ready for some exciting news?"

Ron heard the comment coming over the line and perked up.

"There's a young pregnant woman who lives in Duluth looking for an open adoption for her child," Barbara went on. "She's already gone through your file, and she loves that you live on Mirabelle."

Great. The timing for this couldn't have been worse.

"Apparently, she vacationed with her family on the island when she was a little girl," Barbara said. "Remembered it as being the most magical place she's ever visited. She wants to meet you."

"She does?" Missy glanced at Ron. No one had ever wanted to meet her before today. This was the closest she'd been to adopting a child since she'd begun the process.

Excited, Ron squeezed her shoulder and then did a little happy dance.

"Yep," Barbara said. "She just came to me last week. After scouring through our files, you're the only prospective parent she likes."

Because of the agency's extensive background check, Missy had been forced to come clean about her family, but they had promised absolute confidentiality and had agreed not to share Missy's identity with anyone. She didn't want her bank balance influencing this process.

"Why me?" Missy asked.

"Get this." Barbara chuckled. "She's a vegetarian, too."

"She has no problem with me being a single parent?"

"Not at all. She seems to respect the fact that you've had to deal with the death of your husband."

Shit. The real question was what was she going to think when she learned that Jonas was still alive, *and* they'd be filing for divorce?

"What's your schedule like over the next couple weeks?"

Missy bit her lip. "Well, it's kind of hectic here," she said, stalling. "Tourist season has started."

Confused by her reaction, Ron cocked his head at her.

"Missy, this is a critical time," Barbara said. "You name the date, but can you come to Duluth?"

Missy tried formulating a better excuse for holding off, but nothing made sense.

"Missy, what's going on—?"

"Okay, fine. I'll come to Duluth. Next week."

"Good. I'll call you with the specifics." Barbara paused. "And, Missy? This young woman is five-months pregnant. She plans on making a decision soon. You could be a mother in only a few months."

Missy hung up the phone and held back the sudden rush of tears threatening to undo her. Five months pregnant. Five months. She glanced at Ron, wishing she could talk to someone about Jonas.

"Did I hear what I thought I heard?" he asked. "You could be a mother by Christmastime?"

Missy nodded, feeling dazed. "That's what she said."

"Holy smokes! That means I could be a grandpa!" Ron muttered. He might not be blood, but he was the closest thing Missy had ever had to a real father. "I gotta tell Jan!"

"No, that's not—"

Ron was already out the door and heading quickly down the alley. As Missy watched Slim scamper after him, she felt her life spinning even more out of control.

She could have a baby in a few months' time. She might finally—finally—be a mother, but the timing couldn't have been more wrong. This was all Jonas's fault. Life had been just fine before he'd collapsed on her doorstep.

I'll bet you didn't even cry.

The memory of his accusation that morning came out of nowhere. How could one man be so wrong? She'd not only cried at his funeral, wreck that she'd been, she almost hadn't made it to the ceremony. Barely able to hold herself upright, she'd sobbed, for what could've been, what should've been, what they'd had and ruined, and for what would never, ever be.

She'd cried all over again for the baby she'd miscarried only a few weeks before he'd died and had never told him about, ached to have a piece of him with her after he was gone. She may have been the one to file for a divorce, but it'd had nothing to do with no longer loving the proud and oh-so-responsible Jonas Abel.

If anything, she'd loved him too much.

CHAPTER SIX

JONAS FELT LIKE AN ASS. Threatening Missy with exposing her past to the people of Mirabelle didn't sit well. He'd had no choice, he reasoned. With Delgado's men after him, possibly FBI as well, he'd have made it one, maybe two days on his own.

As he walked into Missy's kitchen, his regret faded at the sight of the legal document lying on the middle of the counter. The divorce papers. As he flipped through the agreement, any shred of doubt he may have had with regard to her intentions disappeared. She'd signed it four years ago. All he had to do was add his John Hancock and it'd be a done deal. But not today. Swiping up the thing, he stuffed it into his laptop bag.

Having slept the entire morning after Missy left for work, he'd regained some of his energy. At least he was able to maintain his balance as he moved about. After grabbing some toast, he managed a shower and a half-assed change of the dressing on his wound. Then with his gun next to him on the sofa table, he sat on Missy's living room couch, staring at his laptop screen and rifling through the files stored on his memory stick.

Almost from day one of this undercover operation Jonas's superior, Mason Stein, had been worried about internal leaks. The FBI had been under intense scrutiny due to agents selling evidence, so every detail Jonas and Matthews had accumulated through the years had been kept extremely tight. As far as Jonas knew there were only four men privy to the progress in this investigation: Jonas, Matthews, Stein and Stein's boss, Paul Kensington.

With his legs spread in front of him and his back against the wall, Jonas scanned through the sixteen gigs' worth of data he'd maintained on his own. Names, photos, dates, drop locations, bank records, license numbers, safe houses, suppliers, dealers. Theoretically, it was all useless. He and Matthews had been made, but how?

Moment by moment, Jonas replayed in his mind the details of the days before he'd been shot and could identify nothing of significance. He could not for the life of him pinpoint when they'd nailed him as FBI.

The morning Jonas had gotten shot he'd been woken by a phone call summoning him to a meeting at a local bar. Nothing unusual about that. He'd picked up Matthews and stopped for coffee along the way. As they'd left his car to go into the bar through the rear entrance, a group of men had jumped him and Matthews in broad daylight. He'd recognized all of them. None had been significant players in the operation he and Matthews had been about to take down. But the shots that had killed Matthews and pierced Jonas's side had come from the building above them.

Who was the shooter? And why hide?

They could've busted this operation wide-open months ago, but they'd been waiting to nail Delgado, the top dog. He was in Colombia orchestrating a huge shipment of drugs that was supposed to be taking place within the next couple of weeks. It was too much of a coincidence that the shit had hit the fan just before they'd planned on nailing the son of a bitch.

Knowing he couldn't use his cell phone, let alone a landline to make any calls, Jonas pulled out one of the untraceable booster phones he'd bought, dialed into an encryption center and then connected with his personal cell phone center. He had three messages.

Number one was from Mason Stein. Short and simple. "Where are you? Matthews is dead. You gotta come in."

Message number two. Also from Stein. "If you're listening to this, you're alive. Damn, I hope you're alive. We need you, Jonas, if we're still going to bust these guys."

Three. Stein again. "Where the hell are you?"

No. Jonas was not going in. If Stein was mixed up in this mess, the longer he thought Jonas dead, the better.

For the first time in Jonas's life, he was going to disobey a direct order. For the first time in his career with the Bureau, he didn't know who to trust. He tried imagining his life without the FBI. Who would he be? Where would he go? What the hell would he do?

Only one thing was for sure. Today wasn't going to bring any answers. Frustrated, he glanced up from his laptop and took in the details of Missy's house. He'd never seen anything like it. The place looked clean, but cluttered.

A desk, the type of place that most would have used to organize bills and mail, housed stacks of unorganized paperwork. Magazines and junk mail were mixed in with old letters and bills, loose photographs in with receipts. Lists were taped and tacked all over the surface.

As for the rest of the first floor, every wall was painted green, brown or gold, but there didn't seem to be any rhyme or reason coordinating the colors. That was Missy for you.

If she liked the colors, she was going to have them, whether or not the combination looked good. Funny, but the rooms looked okay to him.

Live plants were everywhere, hanging in windows, sitting on sills, end tables and counters. Succulents, leafy palms, bushy vines and even a few that flowered, you name a variety of houseplant and it was likely somewhere in her home.

Mats of woven sticks or rugs probably just as eco-friendly covered her bamboo floors. He ran his hands along the side of a bookcase. Figures. As in her bedroom, she'd mixed antiques with modern designs, and wicker and metal with everything, as if she couldn't decide on a set theme.

Leave it to Missy. He shook his head and smiled. If it wasn't nontoxic, sustainable, organic, recycled or all of the above, it had no business being in her house, touching her skin, or going in her mouth.

Surprisingly, as he continued to glance around, some of the tension he felt in his shoulders seemed to leave his body. Her carefree attitude was one of the things about Missy that had initially attracted Jonas, but ultimately one of the things that had forced a wedge between them.

He flashed on coming home after spending two weeks in training out in Quantico and finding their apartment empty. The sinking feeling he'd had in his stomach hadn't been unlike the feeling he'd had as a kid coming home from school one day to find they'd been kicked out of their house. The bank had foreclosed.

But no. He was the only man he knew whose wife had spontaneously gone out and bought a house. With a check. He'd had enough in savings at the time—even more now— that he, too, could've gone out and paid cash for a home.

That wasn't the point. He'd wanted to provide that for her, or at least be involved in the decision. She'd been so ecstatic to have a yard and more room that he hadn't the heart to stand his ground.

You don't pay any attention to me. You're gone all the time. You don't love me.

The accusations she'd thrown at him ripped through his mind. Trying to provide for her by succeeding at his job had been the only way he'd known how to show his feelings for her. So in the end it'd turned out she was right. He didn't know how to love her.

Shaking off the unproductive thoughts, he shifted in the chair and was immediately reminded of the bullet wound in his side. He might like to think he was tiptop, but he wasn't. Even worse than the pain was the feeling of weakness. Too weak to fight, too weak to run, too weak for much of anything.

Food would help. He hated being hungry. Setting his laptop aside, he eased himself off the couch and made his way slowly into the kitchen. He opened Missy's refrigerator and rummaged through the shelves. Fruits and veggies, organic of course. He grabbed an apple, took a bite and chewed as he searched for something a bit more filling. Tofu. Not going to cut it.

Closing the door, he went from one cabinet to the next. Whole grain this and that. Sticks and weeds, all of it. It sure would help his medical condition if Missy had some freaking meat in this house. After the amount of blood he'd lost, he needed iron. Big-time.

At least she wasn't a vegan. He'd noticed a carton of eggs in the fridge. He toasted some bread and fried four brown shelled, free-range eggs that had apparently been hand selected from an actual nest and was just finishing eating when he heard the back door open.

Pulling the gun from his waistband, he moved as quietly as he could to the hallway leading to Missy's bedroom. He held the gun to his chest and waited.

Movement registered in his peripheral vision and he glanced up. The outline of a man's figure reflected in the glass front of a picture in the living room. Whoever it was knew his way around the place.

Jonas hazarded a glance around the corner. *Old man. Sixty-something. Cat trailing him. Must know Missy.* There was no way that Jonas, in his injured state, could move swiftly enough to hide. He stuffed the gun back in his sweats and slowly walked out toward the living room, stretching a bit as he went, feigning a sleepy and nonthreatening state.

"What the…" the man said, stopping in his tracks. "Who are you?"

"Whoa! I might ask the same of you."

"I live next door. Ron Setterberg." He pointed at a hair dryer sitting on the counter. "I was just dropping that off for Missy."

The man had keys. Interesting.

"Your turn," the guy said.

The cat jumped onto the counter, sniffed at Jonas's dirty plate, and tentatively licked at some yolk.

"I'm a…" Who was he supposed to be? Buying himself some time, he picked up the cat and petted him. "Just visiting," he said, being as vague as possible. "Came in late last night. Missy wasn't expecting me."

The man glanced warily at him. Who could blame him? With long hair, a scruffy beard and unkempt clothing,

Jonas very likely looked like a bum. He had a feeling that the cat liking him was the only thing saving him.

"Go ahead and call Missy. You won't offend me."

Without taking his eyes off Jonas, Ron pulled a cell phone out of his back pocket and hit a button. Apparently, Missy was on speed dial. Even more interesting. "Missy, hon? I dropped the blow-dryer off at your house, and there's a man here." The guy paused and listened as he narrowed his eyes at Jonas. "He's your *brother?*"

Brother. Jonas barely kept himself from laughing out loud. That was probably the funniest damned thing he'd heard in months. He and Missy looked about as much like siblings as an AK-47 and a Browning 9mm, and his thoughts about her weren't even close to brotherly.

"All right. If you say so." The man disconnected the call and stuffed the phone into his pocket. Then he sighed and ran his hand slowly down his cheek. He didn't believe Missy, and Jonas had to give the guy credit for that. Still, he clearly cared enough about her to not make a scene.

Jonas let the cat jump to the floor. "I'll only be here a few weeks," he said, trying to put the other man at ease.

"Missy's a very special person. Means a lot to many people on this island."

She certainly did have a way with people. There was no doubt about that. Not wanting to give away his injured state, Jonas stayed where he was while the neighbor headed toward the back door.

"Well, I'm next house on the right if you need anything," he said, standing in the doorway.

If Missy needs anything, is what the man really meant. "That's good to know. Thanks."

Not five minutes later, Jonas heard a key in the lock again. He stood ready, his hand on the gun behind him when a woman barged into the house. She had short, graying hair, and tortoiseshell reading glasses hung from her neck. "I didn't believe it," she muttered to herself. "He told me, but I didn't believe it."

"Can I help you?"

"No, you most definitely cannot." She put her hands on her hips and studied him from head to toe. "I'm Jan Setterberg, Ron's wife."

"Nice to meet you. I'm Missy's bro—"

"Bullshit," Jan interrupted. "Ron's more polite than I am, so I'll come right out and say what he and I are both thinking. I don't know who you really are, but Missy's never mentioned any man in her past other than her husband. And he's dead. So you are quite likely—from the looks of you—nothing but trouble."

Knowing Missy, these neighbors were as important to her as she was to them, so Jonas kept his mouth firmly shut and let the woman have her say. As much as he was messing with Missy's life, it seemed the least he could do.

"Missy's like a daughter to us," Jan went on. "I hope you have her best interests in mind, but if you don't maybe you should leave Mirabelle sooner rather than later." She spun around, letting the screen door slam on her way out of the house.

The cat walked toward Jonas and weaved in and out of his legs. "You like me now, cat, but trust me, that'll change. It always does."

CHAPTER SEVEN

"CAN YOU GET AWAY FOR LUNCH?" Sarah, full of energy, beelined it toward Missy, although between the haphazardly arranged display shelves and stands of T-shirts and gift cards it was impossible to find a straight line through the gift shop.

"Um, yeah, I think I can manage," Missy said, still a little preoccupied with Ron's phone call inquiring about Jonas. "Gaia?" she called to her assistant. "I'm off to get something to eat. Want me to bring anything back for you?"

"A salad would be chill," Gaia said, tying a colorful scarf around her dreadlocks. "But let me get—"

"Nope. I'm buying." Technically, Missy couldn't even afford to pay an assistant's wages based on the sales the gift shop generated, let alone buy an employee lunches, but Missy did it anyway at every possible opportunity. "Save your money for school."

"Thanks, Missy."

Missy grabbed her purse, nothing more than a wallet on a leather strap, and followed Sarah outside. The moment the afternoon sunshine hit her face, she sighed. "Perfect timing. I needed this break."

"Ron told me you heard from the adoption agency this morning." Sarah glanced at her expectantly.

That was fast. She couldn't help but wonder if he'd told Sarah anything else, like the fact that a man was staying at her house.

"I'm so excited for you!"

"Don't hold your breath, Sarah. All kinds of things could go wrong."

"But this is the closest you've ever been."

"Which is why I'd prefer not talking about it," Missy said.

Sarah glanced sideways at Missy and opened her mouth.

"I think it's your pick today," Missy said, butting in. "Where do you want to go?"

"All right, fine. I'll let it go." Sarah shook her head. "But I want to be the first to hear about any new developments."

"Deal."

"Let's go to the Bayside. We haven't been there for a while."

Although Missy's favorite restaurant on the island was Duffy's Pub, given the variety of vegetarian options Erica Taylor had added to the menu, she could find something to eat anywhere. They'd taken no more than a few steps down the street when Missy blurted out, "What would you do if someone you care about had kept something from you?"

Sarah glanced at her. "I guess that depends."

"On what?"

"What she lied about."

"Keeping something from someone isn't really a lie, is it?"

"Sure it is. A lie of omission."

Exactly what Jonas had claimed. Missy looked away. No one understood.

"What have you lied about?" Sarah asked.

"Me? What? I…"

"Missy, you're about as transparent as that window over

there." Sarah pointed to the ferry office a short distance from the pier.

Missy closed her hand over the protective crystals hanging from her leather-banded necklace. Before she could admit the truth about her family or her past, they'd reached the Bayside and Hannah Johnson, one of the island's only elementary school teachers, joined them.

"Hey," Hannah said. "That was good timing."

"No kidding," Sarah said. "You must be psychic."

Missy glanced at the two of them and grinned. "Oh, shut up." Teasing her about her untraditional beliefs and life-style had become a favorite pastime for her friends. "Sarah, you called Hannah before you left your shop, didn't you?"

"Busted." Hannah grinned.

They were all laughing as they walked into the café. As Hannah moved ahead of them to take a table by the window, Sarah whispered to Missy, "We'll talk later, okay?"

Missy nodded. As they ordered and chatted, Missy began feeling nostalgic about her life on Mirabelle and how everything could change depending on what happened with Jonas. There were several locals having lunch who waved in greeting when they noticed her group.

Police Chief Garrett Taylor and his deputy, Herman Stotz, sat at the counter. Shirley Gilbert, who ran a bed-and-breakfast, sat at a nearby table lunching with Mary Miller, the candy shop owner and Charlotte Day, the librarian. Doc Welinsky, retired now, sat with Dan Newman, the grocer. Carl Andersen, owner of the Rock Point Lodge, sat at another table with his parents, Jean and John, the island pastor. There were others, too, all of whom Missy knew by name.

Some islanders had welcomed her more easily than

others, but most had been friendly from the beginning. These were salt of the earth type people, from unassuming backgrounds, people who lived modestly. Used to be not much changed on Mirabelle. Not so anymore.

Sally McGregor dying from cancer a while back had brought a new permanent postmaster to Mirabelle, Al Richter, a man just as cranky as Sally, but half as lovable. It was no surprise he was sitting alone at the counter. Then, too, the recent boom in Mirabelle tourism due to the pool and golf course had brought several new business owners and charter fishing operations and made it possible for Marty and Brittany Rousseau to expand the Mirabelle Island Inn. They'd added two wings, one for additional guest rooms and the other housed a full-featured spa. But that wasn't all.

Harry Olson had opened a real estate office and was buying up some of the state land in the hopes of building townhomes. Tom and Carolyn Bent had built a nightclub out near Rock Point that had turned out to be even more controversial than the pool and golf course. While some maintained a nightclub brought an unwelcome party element to the island, others claimed the live entertainment running late into the night filled a void in Mirabelle's otherwise family-oriented atmosphere.

As far as Missy was concerned, it would take a lot more than a few new people and businesses to change the heart of Mirabelle. She was only halfway listening to Sarah complain about the bride for an upcoming wedding going nuclear when Sean came into the restaurant. He was heading toward the counter when his gaze landed on her. Immediately, he detoured to their table. "Hello, ladies."

"Hi." Missy smiled uncertainly at him. *Don't say anything about Jonas. Please.*

"Hey, Sean." Sarah stabbed a French fry with her fork and dunked it in some ketchup. "Want to join us?"

Sean hesitated. "Actually, I needed to talk to Missy for a minute."

"Come on," Sarah said. "Sit down." She scooted in to make room for Sean.

Though clearly reluctant, he sat and ordered as if he was in a hurry. The conversation at their table remained light and innocuous, but Sean was clearly preoccupied. The moment Sarah's and Hannah's attentions were distracted by a tourist causing a commotion with a complaint on a bill, he handed Missy a sample bottle of medicine.

"Antibiotic," he whispered. "I didn't have enough to leave with you last night."

"Thank you."

"How is he?"

"How's who?" Hannah asked, spinning back to them.

Sean said nothing, only waited for Missy.

"Um…my brother," Missy said.

The Mirabelle islanders were a nosy lot. Even if Jonas stayed inside, as she'd asked him, one of her neighbors was sure to notice someone in her house while she was working. Lights going on and off or his shadow in a window. Besides, with Ron already happening upon Jonas, it was probably best to get his presence out in the open.

"What?" Gape-mouthed, Sarah stared at Missy. "A *brother?*"

"You've never said anything about a brother," Hannah added.

"We're not very close." She'd never said anything, period, about a family and who could blame her. She had nothing in common with any of her real siblings.

Last Missy had heard, from the occasional news report or celebrity profile, her brother, the oldest, was following in their father's political footsteps. Her sister, only a few years older than Missy, was a force in her own right on Wall Street. And the baby of the family was in rehab for a recurring addiction to painkillers when he wasn't practicing corporate law.

"So is that what you were talking about?" Sarah asked. "This whole keeping something from someone business?"

Not knowing what else to do, Missy nodded.

"Don't worry about it." Sarah waved it off. "Sounds like you weren't expecting his visit."

"No," Missy said. "He kind of surprised me."

"Must be a family trait." Hannah smiled. "Spontaneity."

"You could call it that."

"Yeah, but is he cute?" Sarah asked, grinning.

"Depends how dark you like your men," Sean quietly offered.

"The darker the better."

"Then you're in luck."

"Oooh." Sarah fanned her face. "You two must be as different as night and day."

Yeah, that pretty much summed it up. "Jonas is adopted," Missy said, digging her hole even deeper, but no one would ever believe Jonas shared even a teaspoon of Missy's blood.

Sean gave a short shake of his head and looked away.

"What?" Sarah asked, looking back and forth between Missy and Sean. "What's going on?"

"Nothing," Missy said, stabbing some romaine off her plate and quickly stuffing it in her mouth.

"How did you manage to meet Missy's brother before us?" Hannah asked.

"Right place at the right time, I guess," Sean said.

"So when do we get to meet him?" Hannah asked, Sean's sarcasm zooming full speed over her head.

"Oh, it's—"

"I have to work tonight," Sarah said, her wheels turning. "Why don't you bring him along to happy hour tomorrow night?"

"I don't—"

"That's a great idea," Hannah interjected. "Missy, you can't keep him all to yourself."

As if she'd want to. In fact, she'd been planning on staying away from her house as much as possible until Jonas vacated the premises. There was no way she was bringing him to Duffy's.

CAREFULLY, JONAS EASED the padding off his bullet wound and a jolt of pain seized him. He sat on the edge of the bed and gritted his teeth. Missy's doctor boyfriend had said the dressing should be changed at least once a day, but the mandate was proving difficult to manage on his own.

The cat, who had been following Jonas around for the past hour, batted at a piece of string dangling from his bandage. Jonas reached out to pet him and felt the pain in his side dim ever so slightly. "What do you want with me?"

The front door opened, and he reached for his gun on the bedside table. Keys landed on the counter. Missy. Her gift shop had to have closed up hours ago, so he had no doubt she was trying to avoid him.

Too bad.

"Missy?" he called, setting the gun down. "I need your help."

"With what?"

"My bandages."

Her slow footsteps sounded down the hall. "Where are you?"

"Upstairs." Refusing to sleep in her room again, he'd moved all his things to the guest bedroom.

She came up the steps. Tentatively, she glanced into the room. Her gaze skittered away from his bare chest to take in the medical supplies he'd set out on the bed. When she saw the cat lying next to him, she said, "I thought you didn't like cats."

"He doesn't seem to appreciate that fact." Jonas pushed the damned thing off the bed and then motioned at the bandages. "I can't do this myself."

Sighing, she walked into the bathroom and washed her hands. On her return, she ordered, "Lie down."

Without a word, he complied, easing himself onto his back with his wounded side closest to the edge of the bed. Her hands touched his skin and he closed his eyes, waiting for the inevitable. Any minute, she'd no doubt rip off what remained of the tape stuck to his skin. He tensed.

Instead, to his complete surprise, she gently eased off the bandage. He should've known she wouldn't intentionally hurt him. Not Missy. Missy with the gentle touch. Missy, whose hands had been the first thing that had drawn him in.

He swallowed, trying to take his mind off the first night he'd met her. "So I'm your brother, huh?"

"That's the best I could come up with."

"Who's adopted?" he asked, chuckling. "You or me?"

"You." Her hands paused in their work, remained still on his skin. Soft. Warm. The heat of Missy's hands sank deep below the surface of his skin.

To this day, Jonas had never felt anything quite like the

feeling of her touch on his body. As if they were somehow one with each other, she and she alone had the uncanny ability to calm or arouse him with one touch. With one touch he knew her thoughts, her feelings. Since the very first night they'd met, it'd been that way between them.

Against his will, the memory came back to him in one sudden rush. She'd been reading trot cards at a hole-in-the-wall bar in Quantico. All of the other agents he was with had wanted to take their turn getting a reading. What they'd really wanted was a chance with her out back, but she was quite clearly not interested in any of them.

He'd kept his distance, watched and waited. Something about her had made him uneasy. She believed that tarot stuff and had freaked out a couple of the other agents. More than once she'd caught Jonas's assessing gaze, and more than once she'd held his gaze longer than most people would've been comfortable with. Her eyes said one word and one word only to Jonas. *Sex.*

When she'd finished readings for the rest of the guys in his group, someone pushed him into the chair. He sat in front of her, drained his beer and waited. Without a word, she looked into his eyes, set the cards aside and took his hands. Pressing her fingers over his, she opened his palms and studied them. The guys laughed and joked about it.

"You readin' his love line or his life line?"

"He gonna win a lottery?"

"Careful, sweetheart, you don't know where those hands have been."

Jonas didn't crack a smile. All he could do was watch her. After being unable to goad either him or her into a reaction, the other agents gradually lost interest and wandered closer to the bar for more beer. Once they'd been left alone, he leaned forward and whispered, "What do you see?"

As if snapped out of a trance, she'd glanced up. "What did you say?"

"I asked what do you see?"

"Ah…nothing."

"Liar." She never did tell him what she'd found so interesting about his hands.

"You can't really read palms the way people think," she whispered, her gaze moving slowly over his face.

"Then why are you looking?"

"Yes," she'd said out of nowhere.

"What?"

"I said, yes, let's go somewhere else."

He'd stood, grabbed her hand and, as quietly as possible so as not to draw attention to either of them, pulled her outside. The cool night air had no sooner hit his face than she'd pushed him against the building, jumped into his arms and kissed him.

With a hard-on growing harder every second, he carried her to his SUV in the far part of the lot, opened the back door and lowered the seats. None of this backseat bullshit. He'd wanted her good and laid out under him, even banged his forehead in his rush to join her inside.

"Condoms," she whispered, as he closed them inside the vehicle. "I don't have any."

"You don't?" Breathing hard, he studied her face. "You've never done something like this before, have you?"

"No." She shook her head.

Somehow that had made him want her all the more. He'd kissed her again, hard, and then broke away briefly to fumble in his glove box for the box of condoms. What followed was sweaty, mind-blowing sex. The kind guys only fantasized about. Then they'd moved from his SUV to her apartment a few miles away for more of the same. It was hours before they'd bothered asking each other's names. The following morning, they'd exchanged numbers amidst promises to see each other again that night and the next and the next.

One week had turned into two. Two into twelve. Those had been the most perfect nights of his life. Being with Missy, feeling her under him, learning, touching, tasting every inch of her body.

As her fingers moved again, bringing him back to the present, he tensed with an instantaneous hard-on. She eased what was left of his old bandage off his skin and he opened his eyes. His gaze landed on the tattoos on the underside of her left arm. Those were new. A line of small black Sanskrit symbols not normally visible, but damned sexy. He might've enjoyed running his tongue along that soft, tender skin.

He closed his fingers around her wrist and held out her arm for a better look. "What's with the tattoos?" he murmured, his voice thick.

"You wouldn't understand."

"No?"

She pulled against his grip, and then stilled, her strength no match for his. "Let me go, Jonas."

"If you say so." He held her a moment longer and she closed her eyes. Her breathing escalated. She licked her lips and swallowed as she, too, was remembering. Before thinking better of it, he drew her toward him.

She came, unresisting as if mesmerized, as if she had no clue what she was doing. When her lips were a hairbreadth from him, her eyes popped open. She jumped back, yanking on his arm. The strain caused a jolt of pain through his side, but he held her tight. "Too bad I've got this gunshot wound or we could…revive a memory or two from old times."

"Over my dead body."

"Scared, Missy?"

Her eyes darkened, darted down his bare chest and then back to his face.

"You still want me. You know you do. I know you do. Where's the problem?"

"The problem is that you haven't changed. You're still the same man, Jonas." Her breath puffed out of her in little pants. "A man who'd choose taking a call from his boss over time with me. An out of town assignment over time with me. Death over trying to make our marriage work. I never was a priority in your life, and I never could be."

He released her arm and looked away.

Throwing the cotton gauze onto the bed, she stalked out of the room. "From now on change your own damned bandages."

CHAPTER EIGHT

THE NEXT DAY WAS ONE LONG string of tourists in and out of Whimsy. As dinnertime approached and the crowds thinned, Missy left Gaia in charge and walked down Main toward Duffy's Pub for her standing happy hour date with friends. Going home to freshen up first was not an option. After what had happened last night when Jonas had asked for help changing his bandages, she wasn't going to risk being near the man.

God help her, but he'd been right. After everything he'd put her through, she still wanted him, wanted to feel his mouth pressing against hers, his arms around her, his body over her. Well, she might be stuck with him living in her house for a few weeks, but that didn't mean she had to go home any more than was absolutely necessary.

The moment she opened the pub door, the sounds of laughter and classic rock from the jukebox greeted her. Erica Taylor, the police chief's wife, was working the main bar. Normally, Erica cooked, but occasionally she took a break from the kitchen and bartended. It gave her a chance to visit. Tonight the tables in the restaurant were full. Groups of people either spilled out onto the sidewalk or hung out in the pub waiting to be seated. Missy squeezed past them and took a seat at the less popular end of the bar, saving a few extra spots. "Hey, Erica."

"Hey, yourself."

"Who's watching little David tonight?"

"Garrett's at home with Jason and the baby," Erica explained. Erica had gotten custody of her nephew, Jason, when Erica's sister had been murdered by her abusive husband. Despite the awful circumstances, the boy seemed to be adjusting well to Mirabelle. "He might bring the boys down later tonight."

"Oh, good. Haven't seen them all for a while."

Erica frowned as she studied Missy. "You look tired."

"It's been a long couple of days."

"Anything I can do to help?"

"You can get me a big glass of zin and an order of your fantastic bruschetta."

"Coming right up."

Erica had no sooner set a wineglass filled with dark, rich red wine than Sarah came into the bar and took the seat next to Missy. As the worried expression on Sarah's face registered, Missy asked, "What's the matter?"

"I'll tell you in a minute," Sarah said, turning her attention to Erica. "Bartender, bring me a dirty martini. ASAP, please!"

Erica raised her eyebrows. "Tough day?"

"One of the worst ever."

"Then I'll make it a double."

Missy turned toward Sarah. "What happened?"

"Remember I was having problems collecting five thousand dollars from the couple who had that no-holds-barred wedding earlier this month?"

"Yeah."

"Well, the collection agency said the bride and groom have virtually fallen off the face of the earth."

"Have you contacted any of the guests?"

"No one knows for sure where the couple went. They think they left the country to trot around China. I might never see a dime."

"That doesn't seem possible." Missy could bail Sarah out of this financial mess in a heartbeat with money from her trust fund. Still, she hesitated.

"I put in weeks planning that deal." Sarah shook her head. "I still owe the Mirabelle Island Inn for the cost of the banquet room, the meals and the week the couple stayed in the honeymoon suite."

Missy opened her mouth and then quickly shut it. This wasn't the first time she'd had the urge to help out. More than once she'd wanted to figure out some way to anonymously send her friend some money, but in the end she couldn't figure out anything that wouldn't arouse Sarah's suspicions.

Missy fiddled with the stem of her wineglass. "Marty Rousseau will work out a deal with you, won't he?"

"Yeah, but I can't ask him to share in the loss. It's not his fault I got stiffed. I had to ask Ron for a few extra weeks to get my rent to him."

"He and Jan will understand."

"I still don't like being in this situation."

"You'll have to put off buying a house, won't you?"

"For at least another year." Sarah nodded. "I was eyeing that little cottage by your house."

It wasn't that Missy felt stingy with her money. Not in the least. But there was a difference between helping out a college student like Gaia by paying for hours worked and giving a friend a handout. Missy had given money to friends in the past. Invariably, the relationship changed. Sarah's friendship was too important to risk.

Missy covered Sarah's hand. "You'll get there."

"I guess there are worse places to live than the apartment above the flower shop, but Brian was really looking forward to having a yard."

Erica returned with a very large ice-cold martini filled with several toothpicks of olives. "I want to know what's going on," Erica said, setting the drink down. "But the bar's starting to fill up."

"Don't worry about it," Sarah said. "I'll no doubt be moaning about this for weeks." Then she took a deep breath and smiled. "Definitely not for the rest of this night, though."

Sarah was taking a big sip of her drink as Hannah came in and took the seat on Missy's other side. "So, Missy, where's your brother?" Hannah asked.

"Oh, yeah, I forgot about that!" Sarah said. "That'll brighten my day."

Missy took a gulp of wine. "Um. He wasn't feeling well, so he couldn't come."

Hannah's shoulders slumped. "Well, that sucks."

Sarah narrowed her eyes at Missy, but didn't say a word.

Hannah ordered a chardonnay, and over the course of the next hour the bar area filled completely with both locals and tourists. Ron and Jan Setterberg as well as Sean had come to join their group.

The moment Hannah and the others were occupied with a story Jan was telling about something that had happened at the Mirabelle Island Inn that afternoon, Sarah leaned over to Missy and whispered, "So what's the deal with this brother of yours?"

"What do you mean?"

"You don't want us to meet him. Why?"

"It's…a strange situation."

"Best friends can handle even the most convoluted of problems."

This was Missy's opportunity to tell all, and if they hadn't been in Duffy's she might have gotten the ball rolling. As it was, the conversation was loud, the music louder. "I know we need to talk, but not here, not now, okay?"

"All right, but don't think I'm letting you off the hook for good." Sarah turned back to listen to Jan's story.

A short while later, Garrett Taylor came into Duffy's, bringing with him Brian, Jason and David, his and Erica's four-month-old baby. Brian ran over to give Sarah a hug.

"All those kids." Missy grinned at Garrett. "How did you get to be so lucky?"

He chuckled. "You want 'em, you got 'em."

"Be still my heart!" Missy held out her arms for David, who quickly honored her with a gummy smile the moment he was in her arms.

"Garrett," Sarah said. "Thanks for watching Brian."

"No problem." Garrett turned, caught Erica's gaze and winked.

Missy turned away from the sudden intimacy that developed between Garrett and Erica and sighed. She wasn't sure if she and Jonas had ever been that contented in their short marriage.

Steering her thoughts from Jonas, Missy turned back to David, kissed his chubby cheek, nuzzled his neck, and took a good whiff of that wonderfully clean-smelling baby skin. It was so hard to hold an infant and not think of her own miscarriage. The easiest thing in the world would've been to avoid children all together, but it wasn't her way.

Instead, she had sleepovers with Sarah's son, Brian. Took

Natalie Quinn's kids on overnight camping trips at the island's state park. Even babysat for Sophie and Noah Bennett's twin toddlers on occasion. She had no clue how long it was going to take to adopt a child, so she'd decided long ago to enjoy other people's children as much as possible.

"You look ready for one of those yourself," Sean said, watching her.

A rush of adrenaline ran through her at the thought of the very pregnant young woman Barbara had called about the other morning. They still hadn't set an exact meeting date for next week, but Missy knew she would make that trip to Duluth. "Yeah," she said, grinning. "I guess I am. How 'bout you?"

He laughed. "Never in a million years."

JONAS IMPATIENTLY FLICKED OFF his laptop. Still no news of the shooting. He turned on the TV, watched a minute, maybe two of network news and then snapped off the power. Standing abruptly, he paced the length of the house. His gaze landed on the phone. *Don't do it.*

Forcing his gaze toward Missy's bookshelves, he glanced at the titles. There were one or two bestsellers in fiction, but Missy read mostly nonfiction, always had. Organic gardening. Yoga. Green housing. Not that Jonas was about to pick up a book and read. That'd be the day he could make it through anything longer than a magazine article, especially as stir-crazy as he felt at the moment.

He might be feeling better physically, but that brought on an entirely new problem. All he wanted was to get back to Chicago and wrap up this case, and that'd be the worst thing he could do right now. Every asshole on the street would be on the lookout for him. FBI or not, no one double-crossed Delgado and lived to tell about it. The sooner he put that bastard behind bars, the better.

Stalking into the kitchen, he opened the refrigerator and stared inside. Damn. He'd practically eaten Missy out of house and home, and he'd had enough eggs to choke a gorilla. What he needed was meat. Forced to satisfy the grumbling in his stomach with a measly apple, he shut the door in disgust. It was just too damned bad that Missy didn't want him to leave her house.

While chewing on the fruit, he closed his laptop and set a pencil on top of the unit, the eraser end pointing downward, the opposite of how most people usually positioned a pencil. He could hide the laptop but he figured it was better to know whether or not his info had been compromised than to wonder.

Then he went to Missy's bedroom and pulled two feathers out of her pillow. The chances of someone tracking him here this quickly were slim to none, but there was no point in taking unnecessary risks.

After placing one of the feathers on top of the back door, he all but closed the front door before pinching the other feather in the jamb and then very slowly and carefully pulling the door completely closed. He then jammed a baseball cap onto his head, slipped on a pair of sunglasses and made his way slowly down the hill toward Mirabelle's center.

From here, he had a clear view of the marina. He'd always loved boats, but had never taken the time to pursue that activity. A large boat, decked out with fishing gear, glided into the marina. A charter operation. What a life. But then this whole island was almost too good to be true.

He reached Main and turned onto the sidewalk. Between

the cobblestone streets, meticulous gardens and turreted Victorian bed-and-breakfasts, Jonas halfway expected a knight to come riding on horseback out of the woods. Missy had always had her head high in the clouds, and he couldn't imagine a more perfect place for her to live.

The pay phone at the end of the street filled him with the urge to make contact. "Screw it." He took the disposable cell phone out of his pocket and dialed a sequence of numbers that would make his call untraceable. It was time to shake the tree and see what fell to the ground.

His call was answered after several rings. "Special Agent Stein."

Jonas remained silent, waiting, wondering, not trusting Stein for a second.

"Is anyone there?" After a long pause, he quietly said, "Jonas?"

"Someone needs to take target practice a little more seriously."

The split second of silence that followed was oh, so telling. "Jonas!" Stein said. "You're still alive. Thank God!"

"Don't fuck with me, Mason. You're in on this. I don't know how, but you are."

"What are you talking about?"

Jonas laughed. "I'll figure it out, and then you're going down."

"Dammit, Jonas! Don't hang—" Mason, phone in hand, pounded his desktop in frustration. "Son of a bitch!" He clicked off the one-sided connection and immediately put in a request for an emergency trace on the call, although he knew what they'd find. A short while later he got the results. Dead end. The call had not only been encrypted, it'd been rerouted so many times they'd never be able to determine its origin.

Stein swung around in his chair and stared out of his corner office window. If he didn't come up with something soon, before Abel put the pieces he had into the puzzle, this deal was going to come crumbling down around him.

He dialed a number on his cell and the call was immediately answered. "He's alive," Mason said.

"He just called? Could you trace it?"

"What do you think?" Mason barely held his temper in check. "Why the hell can't you find him?"

"I tracked him heading north out of the city, but his trail goes cold on some back road in Wisconsin."

"Hospitals, doctors? Anyone report a gunshot?"

"No one. With the amount of blood he lost at the scene, I doubt he could've doctored himself."

"Then there's someone you're either ignoring, or don't know about." Mason flipped on the video clip he'd found on file of Abel's funeral all those years ago. He froze on the frame picturing those who had been closest to Abel. Several Bureau men he recognized stood behind Abel's father and widow. "I'm putting a tail on Agents Adams, Reynolds and Steadman."

"They were as close as Abel got to friends. It's possible he'll try to make contact."

"Did you find his father?"

"He's in Florida. I already put a man on his apartment, but I'll bet anything Abel won't go there."

"Have you located his wife yet?"

"I'm telling you that's a dead end. She was in the process of divorcing Abel when we recruited him, remember?"

"Hate? Love? If you ask me she looks pretty shaken up in this funeral footage. How can it be so difficult to locate a civilian? Just track the death benefits."

"She's denied all payments from day one."

That made him pause. "Why?"

"Your guess is as good as mine."

"Hack into their database. Find that woman. I have a feeling she's the key. I'll put one more thing in play on my end. When push comes to shove, it'll only give us a day or two, but that'll be all we need."

SUPREMELY PISSED, JONAS shoved the cell phone in his pocket. He studied the faces of the crowds wandering along the sidewalks and riding bikes along the cobblestone streets. Oblivious, all of them, to the shit going on around them. Especially that mother and father across the street. If they didn't take better care watching their child, the little boy was going to get trampled by one of those horse-drawn carriages.

Not your job. Ignore it. What Jonas needed to take his mind off Stein—and the kid—was a tall, frosty mug of beer and a thick hunk of steak.

The kid stepped off the sidewalk and onto the cobblestone road. A carriage clip-clopped its merry way down the street. Young driver. College kid. Two more steps and—

"Whoa! Whoa! Whoa!" The carriage driver called, spotting the child.

Too late. Brakes weren't holding. A bystander on the sidewalk called, "Watch out!" Jonas shot out into the street. The mother turned and screamed. Jonas dodged a bicyclist and the lead horse, scooped up the kid, and deposited him on the sidewalk.

The carriage slowed to a stop. "Everyone all right?" the driver asked.

"Peachy," Jonas grunted as pain seized him.

"Oh, my God." The mother lifted the little boy into her arms, looking as if she might faint.

"Are you all right?" The father held Jonas's gaze.

Clenching his jaw, Jonas nodded and waited for the pain to subside.

"Thank you," the man said. "Is there some—"

"No. Don't worry about it."

Limping back across the street, Jonas walked up to the first restaurant he ran across, a place called Duffy's Pub. Laughter and music spilled out onto the sidewalk and, not in the mood for people, he almost turned away. Then the scent of garlic and grilled meat wafted toward him from the alley and his stomach made the decision for him.

Inside, he surveyed the crowd. From the dress and paraphernalia, tourists most assuredly mixed with locals at the tables and booths. Immediately, his eyes latched on Missy at the bar, standing next to the good doctor. Knowing her highbrow background, it seemed strange seeing her in this kind of setting, but there was something about a bar that brought out the best in Missy. Laughing and smiling, she looked more gorgeous than the first night he'd met her.

Doctor Sean surely noticed. He was tall, had to lean down to talk in her ear. She laughed at whatever he said and they both looked at something in her arms.

What the—? A baby. So focused on her interacting with the doctor, he'd totally missed the fact that she was holding a little boy. The sight of her smiling at the kid tugged at Jonas's heart in a strange way.

While they'd been married they'd mentioned kids only once. Waiting had been the consensus and she'd seemed content. She was young. She had all the time in the world for children. And him? He'd wanted to be more stable before they went that route. A house. A job that didn't take him out of town or undercover.

Clearly, her vision had changed. She wanted kids. Now.

She glanced at Sean and they laughed together, apparently at something the baby had done. Again, jealousy reared up inside Jonas. He was about to turn around and find another restaurant when she caught sight of him. No way to back out now.

Ignoring the lingering ache in his side, he walked over to where she was standing at the bar. "Hey."

"Hi." When she gripped the crystals on the necklace around her neck, presumably seeking protection from him, he looked away. He'd never wanted to hurt her. He'd truly thought he'd been doing her a favor by dying. Coming back? That he hadn't given much thought, but who could think with a bullet wound in the side?

"Jonas. This is Sarah, Hannah, Sean and Garrett," Missy said, making introductions. "Everyone, this is my brother, Jonas."

He nodded at each person in turn, but the doctor only glared at him. When the Setterbergs joined the group, Jonas straightened his shoulders and prepared himself for a few more dirty looks. There was no point in trying to butter them up with a smile. They already hated him.

"Erica, bring this man a beer," Ron said, patting Jonas

on the back. "He just saved a little boy out front from getting run over by a horse."

As Ron went on explaining what happened, Jonas ducked his head. The last thing he wanted was to draw more attention to himself.

Jan raised her eyebrows at him and whispered, "Guess sometimes there's more to a man than meets the eye."

"I wouldn't count on it," Jonas muttered.

"That's some fast action," Sarah said. "You must be feeling better."

Jonas glanced at the woman, wondering what exactly that comment meant. Missy wouldn't have told anyone about his gunshot wound. "Yeah, thanks, I do feel better," he hedged. "Except I'm starving."

"You can order something from Erica," Garrett said, studying him, taking him apart piece by piece. "My wife."

If that man wasn't a cop, Jonas wasn't Bureau. "Thanks." Jonas turned as the bartender set a frosty mug of beer in front of him and ordered a basket of chicken fingers as an appetizer, as well as a tenderloin steak, complete with a baked potato, green beans and a salad.

From there the group peppered him with questions to which he responded with what he hoped were innocuous half truths. He'd spent most of the past four years lying to infiltrate and then operate amidst a drug cartel. What was one more night?

As soon as the group let up on their interrogation, Missy pulled him slightly aside. "Thank you for saving that little boy."

"Whatever."

"What are you doing here?"

"Maybe if you kept real food in your house, your guests wouldn't need to head into town for a decent meal."

She glanced away.

Jonas felt the stirrings of a long-dormant conscience chew at his stomach. "I'll go someplace else. Sound like a better plan?"

"You can't. Everyone here will think it's odd. Funny, but my girlfriends want to get to know my *brother*."

"Tell them the truth, Miss."

"Why should I? You'll be gone in no time. I still want to live here. In anonymity. In peace."

CHAPTER NINE

OTHER THAN ANSWERING the questions posed to him, Jonas barely said a word the entire night. After finishing eating, leaving not a morsel on his plate, Sarah tried for a while to carry on a conversation with him, but gave up after receiving a series of one word answers.

Missy could practically see Jonas's brain working overtime analyzing her friends and the rest of the crowd, assessing, deciphering and judging with those dark all-seeing eyes. Working. Always working. It didn't surprise Missy for a moment that Jonas had saved a little boy's life. All in a day's work for him. Strung rope-tight, he looked as though he might snap at any moment.

Once upon a time, there used to be a decent, loving man under that cold, hard shell. To bring him out she would've run her hands along his shoulders, or dragged her fingers across his scalp to ease his tension. Plant a gentle, quiet kiss on his cheek. He would've glanced at her and all his worries would've whooshed out of him like a balloon losing air. Then he would've focused all that attention on her. There was no better feeling in the world than being the focus of Jonas's attention.

But that was a long time ago, Missy mused. Another life.

Jonas turned from the bar with his second beer and inadvertently brushed his arm along hers. For a moment, his gaze latched on to hers and it was as if they were alone together in the room, remembering, reliving.

She inched away from him, but the crowd seemed to only push him closer. As if sensing her growing agitation, Sean whispered in her ear, "Come on. Let's dance."

Grateful for the distraction, Missy followed him onto the floor.

"Is it just me, or was the tension getting thick over there?" he asked, smiling.

She chuckled and walked into his arms for a slow rock song.

"How'd you end up marrying that guy, anyway? He doesn't seem like your type."

"No, I suppose not." What was her type? A variety of men had come and gone through Duffy's over the past several years. Golfers, fishermen, old, young, rich, poor. She'd flirted here and there, even dated on occasion, but there'd never once been a man like Jonas.

Sex may have been what had brought her to him, but what had kept her in his arms, what had convinced her to spend the rest of her life with Jonas, had been the way he'd simply let her be. The exact opposite of her father, he'd never once tried to control, direct or change her. Whether she wanted to learn yoga, or how to throw clay pots, taking a cooking class or working at a women's shelter, he'd supported her every move. If only he'd loved her more than his job.

She glanced toward the bar and found Jonas watching her and Sean, his gaze entirely unreadable. He took a long pull on his beer, but his eyes never left the two of them.

Sean spun her around. "Don't look now, but he's watching."

She laughed. Sean could always make her laugh. When they spun back around, Jonas was standing a foot away. Sean stopped.

"I'd like to dance with my…sister, if you don't mind."

Sean glared at Jonas and then glanced at Missy. Jonas never took his eyes off her face.

"It's all right," she said, knowing she'd draw more attention to them by refusing.

Sean stepped back and Jonas immediately took her hand and drew her to the far corner of the floor where they weren't at all visible to her friends at the bar. The song on the jukebox was a new rock song with a fairly fast beat, but he held out his arms for a slow dance.

"No." She shook her head.

"Chicken."

Before she could turn away, he tugged her into his arms and moved half-time, if even, to the beat of the music.

"If I were Sean," he murmured, "there's no way in hell I'd let you dance with me."

"Well, you're not Sean. Not even close."

"He's not your type, Missy."

"Oh, and you are?" She tried to pull away, but the bullet wound apparently hadn't impacted his arm strength. His hold on her was like a vise. He wasn't going to let go.

For a moment, she stopped fighting it. Closing her eyes, she let herself imagine they'd gone back in time to the first few months of their marriage, when they'd been blissfully happy, to a time when his work hadn't yet intruded.

Resting his cheek against the side of her head, he brought her hand to his chest and drew her closer. She felt the solid, but quick thudding of his heart under her hand as his hips pressed against hers, and something warm and liquid and needy fired to life inside her. "What do you want, Jonas?"

"That's simple," he whispered in her ear. "You." His voice was raspy and soft and made her stomach quiver.

"You had your chance."

Before this went too far, she yanked away from him and quickly made an exit along one side of the dance floor. All of her friends at the bar were too busy talking and laughing to notice her heading to the bathroom. She pushed open the door and breathed a sigh of relief that there was no one at the sinks and the stalls were empty, giving her a chance to compose herself. Running her hands under cold water, she splashed her cheeks.

Now what? If she'd known Jonas was going to come here, she would've gone straight home after work. Then again, better late than never. She left the bathroom, planning to quietly exit via the alley, only to find Garrett waiting for her in the hall.

"You all right?" he asked.

"Actually, I'm not feeling all that well. I think I'll head home." She moved toward the rear exit.

"Missy?" Garrett said softly. "I see the way Jonas watches you. If he's your brother, I'm the King of freaking England."

"I'm sorry, Garrett." She turned. "It's…private."

"Just tell me one thing. Are you safe?"

In the way he meant? "Yes. Absolutely."

"Okay then." Garrett nodded. "You need help, day or night, all you got to do is call."

"I know that, Garrett." Guilt over misleading the islanders overwhelmed her. "Thank you." Somehow, someway, she had to find a way to make things right with her friends. Soon. "Will you tell everyone I've gone home?"

"Sure." Garrett went back to the bar.

Missy walked the rest of the way down the hall and pushed through the rear exit. As soon as she closed the door behind her, she took a deep breath and relaxed. Alone. Thank God.

"Going somewhere?" Jonas was leaning against the brick wall of the building, obviously having anticipated her move.

"Home." She took a step toward Main, but he blocked her path. "Don't touch me." She put up her hands to warn him off. If he kissed her, she'd be a goner. His hands, she could maybe fight, but his lips, his mouth on hers? She had no defense against him.

He didn't move. His feet remained planted in the same spot on the cobblestone, but to Missy it felt as if he'd come to stand only inches from her. She could've sworn she felt his breath fan her neck, his heat on her arms.

"Why, Missy?" he breathed. "What are you afraid of?" His gaze moved to her lips. He came toward her and slowly, slowly bent his head toward her. His mouth settled on her forehead. She couldn't have moved if she'd wanted to.

Closing her eyes, her head tilted back as if it were suddenly as heavy as a bowling ball. His lips trailed down her nose. It seemed forever before the first, warm stroke of his lips against her mouth. Then his tongue licked at hers, and a groan sounded. Hers, his, she couldn't be sure.

"We had our chance, Jonas," she whispered. "Everything went bad."

"Not everything." His gaze simmered with memories and she felt herself melting with the heat coming off him. "I know one thing that was always good between us."

"Jonas—"

"No more talking," he said, bending his head toward her.

"All it ever did was get us into trouble." His lips sliding against her cheek and down her neck.

She pressed back against the brick wall, wishing she could slip through it, knowing exactly what was going to happen if she couldn't stop this. She put her hands against his chest, in a ridiculously feeble attempt to push him away. He only laced his fingers through hers and slowly drew her hands over her head. Then he was against her, pressing into her and all she wanted was to be under him, to feel his weight pressing on her.

"We always had this," he murmured against her lips and kissed her. He pushed the line, was insistent, but not needy. Resolute in his movements, but not arrogant.

She tilted her head, unintentionally urging him on and he dipped his tongue inside her mouth, at once testing and teasing. He knew her better than she knew herself, read her body, her touch, her sighs. She would never be able to walk away from him. Not while his hands were on her, not while she wanted him with an ache four years in the making.

Her bones turned liquid, her want quickly spiraled into need. There was only one thing she could do to stop this madness. "No," she breathed, knowing he would never force her.

"You don't mean that."

She closed her eyes and pushed the word from her mouth. "No!"

His hands and lips stilled for a moment. "You're as much mine today, Missy, as you were that first night in Quantico. There's no other man who can make you feel the way I do, and you know it."

She ran her hand over her mouth, trying to dispel the tingling sensation. "Just because you can, Jonas, doesn't mean you should." Summoning every ounce of willpower, she turned and walked swiftly home.

JONAS FOLLOWED MISSY, his thoughts chaotic. At first only a few steps behind her, the dull ache in his side had him falling back a good half a block by the time she reached her house. She went inside, slamming the front door behind her.

He arrived in time to hear her slam her bedroom door. Pacing in the kitchen, he managed only one length of the room before abruptly stopping, a raging hard-on pressing uncomfortably against his jeans.

This need he had for her was eating him up from the inside out, and there was little doubt something very similar was happening to her. Or was it? She was in her bathroom getting ready for bed, washing her face, brushing her teeth as if nothing had happened. How could she possibly put that kiss out of her mind? Since the moment they'd first met and he'd first touched her, Missy had been like a volcano ready to erupt. Nothing had changed for him. How could it have changed for her?

Then it hit him. Nothing *had* changed. She hadn't any more control than him. It was all an act.

Well, maybe it was time to call her bluff.

Stalking down the hall to her bedroom, he turned the knob and pushed open the door. The room was dark. He saw nothing but a sliver of moonlight slicing the room in half. The only sound was a sharp intake of breath. Then his eyes adjusted and his gaze landed on her body. In profile. Naked.

He nearly lost it right then and there.

Instinctively, she pulled the nightgown in her hands in front of her as she spun toward him. "What are you doing in here?" she whispered.

I want you. He didn't have to say it for her to know it. Taking a few slow steps into the room, he gave her a moment to accept the inevitable.

"Stop right there." She held out her hand, exposing one full breast upturned and bathed in moonlight.

Jonas swallowed, aching to draw that dark, tight nipple into his mouth. As soon as he did, she'd be his again. The word *no* would disappear from her vocabulary. "You want this as much as I do, Missy. Admit it. At least to yourself if not to me."

"Maybe I do. Maybe I don't," she whispered, though the sound was more of a whimper. "Sometimes what we want is the worst thing for us."

"Enough talk. Let's do this." He went to her, stood before her and waited for her to step back. When she didn't, he reached out and ran his hand over her collarbone and down her arm, giving her every chance to pull away, to say no again, to back up her words with action. Instead, she closed her eyes and her head fell back, in silent invitation.

He bent toward her and kissed her neck, her shoulder, her arm and then he moved to the upper swell of her breast, giving her every chance to back away and shut him down. Instead, her breathing turned rapid. The nightgown slipped from her grasp and Jonas could no longer hold back. He cupped her bare breast in his hand and took her into his mouth, laving her nipple with his tongue.

"Jonas," she breathed. "Please."

"Please what, Miss?" Tenderly, carefully, he closed his teeth over her nipple. "What do you want me to do?"

She moaned and put her hands on his head, as if she couldn't decide whether to push him away or pull him closer. "I…I don't know," she whimpered.

"I do." Gently, he ran his hands along the sharp slope of her shoulders, down the gentle sweep of her back, and on to the rounded curve of her bottom, cupping her to him.

That's when she touched him, dipped her hand under his shirt and turned hot under his hands.

"Want that off?" He ripped his shirt over his head and threw it on the floor. "Now what?"

She glanced lower.

"Excellent idea." Quickly, he unzipped his jeans and dragged them off, right along with his boxers.

Pulling her into his arms and feeling her naked breasts pressed against him took him back. "This at least was always perfect between us." From the very first time to the last, she'd given him everything she'd had to give. He'd done the same.

He backed her onto the bed, spread himself over her, brought her knees up and felt her softness against his rigid flesh. He hadn't meant to move so fast, but it'd been so long for him and she was so ready, so slick, so swollen. She shifted, tilted her hips under him, putting the tip of him inside her. The uncontrollable need to have her consumed him. He thrust hard, driving himself into her.

"Oh, Missy," he whispered against her mouth. "There isn't a better feeling in the world than being inside you."

The moment Jonas had touched her, the moment he thrust into her, it was as if Missy had ceased to exist, as if her body was no longer her own, as if every hair, every breath, every single one of her bones belonged not to her, but to Jonas. He moved one way and she moved with him, as though she not only anticipated him, she was a part of him.

He brushed his mouth against hers as he drove hard into

her one last time. Their breaths mingled as they came together, as they spiraled into oblivion for several long, blissful moments where not a coherent thought pierced her consciousness. There was only skin and heat and the feel of the only man she'd ever loved inside her, pulsing against her, making her his again.

Slowly, as her orgasm shuddered to completeness, she became aware, limb by limb, of how tightly she'd wrapped herself around Jonas, holding him to her. What was she doing? Suddenly, Missy crashed back to reality. After what he'd done to her, after faking his death and walking away, how could she let this happen?

Ashamed, she drew her legs down and held still. She prayed he would just leave, leave her alone, leave her be, leave her to gather the pieces of herself back together.

He took a shuddering breath, rested his full weight against her for a moment and rolled onto his back. "When I'm right, I'm right," he said with a smile in his voice. "You wanted that as much as I did."

With those words, what little was left of her dignity dissolved. She covered her face with her hands and couldn't stop a tiny sob from escaping.

"Missy?" He reached for her.

"Don't." She rolled away from him. "Don't ever touch me again. Never."

"Missy—"

"No. No, no, no, no, no." Grabbing a T-shirt and sweatpants, she yanked them on and headed for the door.

"Oh, so now you hate me, right?"

She spun back around to find him lying lazily back against her pillows. "The only person in this world I hate more than you right now, Jonas," she whispered, "is me."

THE BACK DOOR SLAMMED and Jonas felt the smile disappear from his face. As his body sank into a deep lull of contentment, his conscience slowly awakened. "You really are an asshole," he muttered into the cool night air. But she'd wanted that as much as he had. She'd wanted him to take her.

Just because you can, Jonas, doesn't mean you should. Her face. The disgust toward him. Herself.

"Screw it!" He threw a pillow across the room. What was done couldn't be undone.

He got out of bed. She shouldn't be outside at night, at least not alone. He hadn't been followed to Mirabelle and it was highly improbable that they'd found him this quickly, but tempting fate was a good way to get dead.

After pulling his clothes back on, he grabbed his gun and went outside. Quietly, he followed her down a path through the woods. She moved slowly, as if her feet were weighted in cement, but he kept his distance. Rustling not a leaf, nor disrupting a branch, he kept his presence unknown. He'd done enough damage for one night. The least he could do was let her think she was alone.

After a while, she broke through the trees and onto the shoreline. Standing quiet for a moment, she lifted her face to the moon. A trail of tears glistened on her cheek, and it was all Jonas could do not to go to her. But he didn't have it in him to comfort her. Not anymore.

"What do you want?" she whispered.

He went still, stopped even breathing. Was there someone else here? Someone he hadn't seen?

"Haven't you had enough, Jonas?"

How she knew he was here he had no clue, but that was

Missy for you. All intuition and insight. No reason or caution, only feelings and actions. "It's not safe out here."

"Not safe. Out here?" She laughed and hugged herself. "Is that supposed to be a joke?" As she glanced at him, he saw himself through her eyes. He didn't like what was there.

What have I become?

Cruel, cold, and unfeeling for starters.

Yes, she'd very definitely wanted him, his body at least, back in her bedroom. He hadn't forced anything on her, hadn't taken anything she hadn't freely given, but he hadn't planned for it to happen in that way.

"I'm sorry, Miss," he said quietly.

She glanced at him. "The Jonas I knew never would've taken advantage of a woman's weakness in that way." She paused, seeming to gauge his sincerity. "Who *are* you?"

"Not the Jonas you married, that's for damned sure."

"What happened to him?"

He'd as much as died for real in that helicopter crash.

Knowing it would still be best to keep his distance, Jonas leaned against a tree and looked out over the dark lake. "Being undercover is…not for every agent. I was good at it. Maybe too good. That's one of the reasons they wanted me for this assignment. When you're undercover you have to, to some degree, forget who you are and become someone else.

"I didn't mind stepping away from my life for a little while," he continued. "A couple days, a couple weeks, it's not a big deal coming back down, fitting back into your regular life. But four years? To tell you the truth, Missy, I'm not sure I *know* who I am anymore."

Moonlight cast a glow on the side of her face, made her

hair look silver. She'd given herself to him, always wholly and completely. What had he given to her? Nothing but pain.

A piece of the old Jonas, a tiny sliver of humanity, snuck back under his skin. "Come back to your house, Missy. Go to sleep. I swear on my mother's grave, I won't ever touch you again."

CHAPTER TEN

MISSY SAT MOTIONLESS on a bench by the shore and stared out over the relatively calm waters of Lake Superior. The sun was barely rising on the horizon as a charter boat cruised out of the marina with a group of early-rising fishermen. Noisy gulls circled the shoreline, cawing and swooping after breakfast. The first ferry of the day was speeding toward Mirabelle. Though aware of all that was taking place around her, Missy felt disconnected from everything.

Jonas reappearing in her life had shaken her world and she couldn't seem to find solid ground on which to stand. Despite having managed to completely avoid him for the last couple of days, the memory of the earth-shattering sex she'd shared with him was ever-present at the edge of her consciousness. She felt a stranger to herself, and it was all his fault.

Or was it?

On Mirabelle, she thought she'd found a place where she fit, a place where she could settle and build a life. She thought she'd found herself. Instead, she'd been living a lie, and if fitting in was based on a foundation of lies, wasn't it inevitable that her world would eventually crumble? There was no way around it. She had unfinished business in her life and, Jonas or no Jonas, only she could tie it all up. How to begin?

By telling the truth.

Before she could back down, Missy quickly climbed the hill, ran past her own home and went directly to the back of the Setterbergs' house. Their inside door was open, leaving only the screen to block mosquitoes and bees. She heard water running in the kitchen sink and voices, but couldn't make out any words.

"Morning," Missy called. "You two up and about?"

A chair scraped across the kitchen floor and Ron appeared. "Well, you're awake early. Come on in."

Missy entered the kitchen that, more and more, felt as comfortable as her own. It wasn't that unusual for her to appear at their house unannounced. In fact, she did so with a great deal of regularity and, with any luck, what she had to say today wouldn't change a thing between them.

Yeah, right. And she was the Dalai Lama.

"Do you want some tea?" Jan asked.

Although they were both coffee drinkers, they kept a stash of green tea for Missy. "I'd love some, thanks." She sat at the old oak table and poured herself a bowl of cereal, topped it with some blueberries and poured skim milk over the top. Normally, she didn't drink milk, but Ron and Jan drew the line at stocking soy products, so Missy adapted when she was at their house.

They chatted about this and that while everyone finished breakfast. She swallowed the last spoonful of her cereal, sat back in her chair and fussed with her tea.

"Might as well come out with it," Jan said. "The longer you wait, the harder it'll get."

Missy took the bag out of her tea, took a sip and framed her words. "For now, can you keep what I'm going to tell you between us?"

They both nodded, and she knew they'd keep their word.

"Okay. Here goes. There are some things I haven't told you about me." Neither Ron nor Jan said a word during her entire long-winded explanation about her family. When she finally finished, she glanced at them. "So that's it. Everything you ever wanted to know about one Melissa Camden—aka Missy Charms."

Ron and Jan glanced at each other and laughed.

Dumbfounded, Missy sat straight. "Why are you laughing?"

Ron quickly sobered. "Sweetheart, we always figured you were running from something. We just didn't know what it was."

"To be honest, we were worried you might be in trouble with the police," Jan said.

"The police?" Missy sat back. "Why?"

"Wouldn't be the first time someone's come to Mirabelle to hide from the authorities," Ron said, probably referring to Erica when she'd been on the run with Jason.

Jan chuckled. "And let's just say you're not exactly traditional."

Missy wasn't sure she wanted to know what that meant. She was simply happy they were taking this so well. "So you're not mad?"

"Why would we be upset?" Jan asked.

"Because I lied to you."

"Because you'd never share anything about your past?" Ron shook his head. "If you'd have wanted us to know, you'd have told us."

"If we'd felt the need to know," Jan added, "we'd have asked."

"So you understand. I have millions of dollars in a trust account."

They glanced at each other.

"Yeah, that's a little strange," Jan admitted. "It doesn't really change anything between us."

"You are who you are, Missy."

Missy couldn't stop tears of sheer relief from falling down her cheeks.

"Oh, honey." Ron patted her hand. "You mean far too much to us for something like this to come between us."

"No harm done," Jan added. "I gotta ask, though. Why is it so important for you to steer clear of your family?"

"It's hard to explain, but I just…they just…acted so differently from how I felt inside it was hard to figure out who I was around them. Does that make any sense?"

"A little. What about now? After all these years on your own?"

Whether or not things had changed for her was something she hadn't thought much about. "Now, I don't honestly know."

"Are they all bad? Even your mother?"

"My father was the worst to be around, but she did what he told her to do."

"Guilty by association?"

"Exactly."

"Somehow that doesn't seem entirely fair."

"Maybe not, but it's really not about what's fair. It's about what I needed to do for myself. Being out from under the shadow of my father is what I needed." She took a deep breath and tried to explain. "He's very controlling. A his-way-or-the-highway man. He was always lecturing me and my siblings about our duty to pay back what we were given. I can still hear his voice in my mind, saying, 'Your great-great-grandfather was one of this country's most influential men. You must do great things with your lives.'"

"That's a lot of responsibility."

"Life, to me, doesn't need to be big and bold to be meaningful. He'd never understand the quiet difference I make by selling only American-made or fair trade products in my gift shop. By trying to be a good friend and neighbor. By buying Mirabelle Island municipal bonds in my trust account." That slipped out before Missy had thought to rein herself in.

Both Ron and Jan glanced silently at her, their eyebrows raised. "So you were the investor who came in at the last minute and saved the plans for the pool and golf course?" Jan asked.

She nodded.

Ron chuckled. "Well, Missy, you helped a lot of people on this island. Whether they know it or not."

"Not me. The money really belongs to my great-great-grandfather. I'd be content with my gift shop." She sighed and glanced back and forth between the two of them. "So you're truly not upset? Not at all?"

He shook his head.

"I'm not sure the rest of the islanders will have the same lack of reaction."

"Oh, no doubt, you'd get a mix." He sighed. "Some who beforehand wouldn't give you the time of day will suddenly want to be your best friend. Some who are friends, won't know how to act around you. Some won't give a damn."

"I'm not sure you should tell everyone, Missy," Jan offered. "But maybe you should at least tell Sarah. And possibly Hannah."

"I can't."

"If they're true friends, they'll understand."

"You don't know what it's like going through life without connections. I wasn't allowed to be friends with kids I shared interests with and the kids I was allowed to do things with I couldn't stand. In college, people I thought were friends really weren't. I don't know what I'd do if I lost Sarah." She took a deep breath and rallied to tell them about Jonas. "There's one more thing you need to know."

"What more could there be?" Jan asked, surprised.

"Has to do with that man at your house," Ron said, holding her gaze. "Right?"

She nodded. "He's not my brother. He's my husband."

They both sat back and listened, their frowns deepening. By the time she finished explaining him, she felt more confused than ever. "So do you have as clear an insight about Jonas?"

Jan shook her head. "I'm not sure I want to touch that one with a ten-foot pole."

Ron sighed. "Me neither."

Even so, Missy felt the answer settle inside her.

Somehow, someway, she had to find the courage to finish all the unfinished business in her life. She had to talk with Sarah. She'd have to call the adoption agency, set the record straight and let the chips fall where they may. And she needed to be done running from Jonas.

Missy gripped the crystal necklace she'd been wearing since Jonas had arrived on Mirabelle and slipped it off. She had to face him head-on. It was the only way she could hope to find herself again and hold her place in this world.

FEELING LIKE A CAGED wild animal, Jonas paced the length of Missy's house. For as much his benefit as hers, he'd been doing his best to stay out of her way for the past couple of days. Merely catching a whiff of her after she'd left her house each morning for work was enough to stir things up for him. Seeing her in the flesh would've most definitely put him into the right-here-right-now mode. That was the last thing she needed from him.

For her part, every day since he'd landed on her door-step, Missy had been leaving early and coming back late in an effort to avoid him. Why it bothered him, he hadn't a clue, but it did. The sooner he got off this miserable island, the better.

Although his gunshot wound was healing well and he was quickly regaining his strength, he was no closer to solving this issue with Stein. He needed some answers. A diversion wouldn't be so bad, either.

Sliding his gun into a shoulder holster and slipping on a jacket, Jonas went outside. The day was overcast and the sun had almost set, but for anonymity's sake, he slipped on a baseball cap and surveyed the perimeter. A few blocks down the hill, people walked along the main street, but except for a man mowing his lawn a few houses away this residential area was deserted. He made his way down the hill slowly, taking care not to stretch his side too much.

People nodded or raised hands in greeting, but Jonas ignored them all, heading instead to the shore. As he walked, he pulled another disposable cell from his jacket pocket, blocked his number and dialed, hoping the old ex-tension hadn't changed.

The call was answered after two rings. "Special Agent Reynolds."

"Louis, I don't have time for lengthy explanations, so let's make this quick."

"Who is this?"

Jonas paused. It was possible the calls of Jonas's friends—if he'd ever really had such a thing—were being monitored. It was even possible he could no longer trust Reynolds, but he had to take this risk. As long as Reynolds didn't know where Jonas was, no harm no foul. In any case, it was better for Louis to figure this out offline. "We need to talk. You know what to do. Be careful." He hung up.

While he waited to call Reynolds back, he sat down on a bench set away from people some distance from the marina and took in the sights at Mirabelle's shore. No wonder this place attracted all kinds of tourists. There was so much to do. People were enjoying sailing, windsurfing, riding Jet Skis, not to mention fishing.

Nice-sized sailboats and yachts were docked amidst the smaller crafts, but none were as large as those he'd seen off Chicago's shores on Lake Michigan, a playground of the Midwestern rich and famous. Even Delgado owned a yacht large enough for a helicopter pad.

Jonas eyed a charter boat in the marina and watched the captain, an old guy, putz with his gear. Not a bad way to retire, if that was your inclination, but Jonas had no intention of ever slowing his pace. He'd die before he'd retire.

Glancing at his watch, he figured he'd given Louis enough time. He dialed the pay phone where Louis would, hopefully, be waiting.

Louis answered on the first ring. "Jonas? Is this you?"

"You alone?"

"Now I am. Someone tailed me out of the office, but I shook the asshole. Is this really you?"

"You know it is, otherwise you wouldn't be in front of the Last Drop coffee shop."

"Jonas, you died. I was at the funeral."

"Staged. For an undercover op."

There was a slight pause on the line as if Louis was assimilating the information. "You couldn't even tell me? The closest thing you had to a best friend. You son of a bitch."

"You know the drill. Besides," Jonas said, taking a deep breath, "I didn't expect to live through this deal, but what do you know? Here I am with a measly bullet wound in my side."

"What happened?"

"I need your help to find out. You in?"

There was a long moment of silence before Louis said, "Tell me what you need me to do."

"First. Who followed you out of the office?"

"I don't know. Never seen him before. He was a pro, though. Took a while to shake him without letting on what I was doing."

Jonas quickly filled his friend in on an abbreviated status of the case, giving him a bit more detail about the Chicago situation. Antsy now, he stood and walked the beach as he talked. "See if you can access Mason Stein's computer files. E-mail me anything you can find labeled Greenland." Jonas gave him the address he'd set up last night, a location he could access without being identified.

"Why Stein?"

"This mission's his baby. Mason and Kensington are the only ones who know I'm alive."

"That's not protocol."

"At the time I didn't give a shit." Jonas had had nothing except a failed marriage on his plate.

"You should've. You really put Missy through the wringer."

Jonas grunted. "Right." He kept walking and found himself on Main.

"I'm not shitting you, man. She was really broken up. At the wake she looked as if she'd been crying for a week straight. The funeral was worse. Your dad had to hold her up for the entire ceremony."

"You must be remembering the wrong man's death."

"I was there, Jonas. I know what I saw. Whatever Missy's reasons were for wanting a divorce, not loving you wasn't one of them."

Jonas hung up his phone. Missy wouldn't have cried over his death. No way. No how. His gaze landed on the name of a gift shop on the other side of the street printed in large, flowing purple letters above the front door. *Whimsy.* Missy's store. Had to be. Avoiding a horse-drawn carriage clip-clopping down the cobblestone, he crossed the street.

The woman was done hiding for tonight.

ANOTHER NIGHT CLOSING HER SHOP. Missy had wanted to go home, to stick with her new plan to stop avoiding Jonas, but Gaia had a date and couldn't stay. She thought about calling Sarah to see if she and Brian might stop in to share some takeout, but it was probably best to steer clear of her insightful best friend until Jonas left Mirabelle.

Instead, Missy sat at her front counter stringing together another bracelet meant for a man. For some reason, men's jewelry seemed to be the only thing she was interested in making these days. This one was jade, a stone that represented good fortune. The last one had been quartz, meant to provide a clear connection to a person's guardian angel. Something Jonas could use.

Jonas again. No matter what she did or didn't do, she couldn't get him off her mind. Only a couple nights and already this was getting old.

Making jewelry with this degree of internal discord was never a good idea. She closed her eyes, searching for a quiet place in her soul. Only there wasn't such a place. It seemed Jonas had touched every piece of her. If only she could confide in Sarah.

"I need to talk to you." Jonas. He was behind her, somehow coming through her front door as quietly as a wolf. From the sound of his voice, he was angry.

Pushing back from the desk, she straightened her shoulders and prepared herself for what she knew would be an onslaught of emotions. She spun around and lost her breath. Nothing could've prepared her for the sight of him. He was so beautiful in this state. Energy and passion vibrated off him in intense waves. Facing the man head-on had just gotten much, much harder.

Good. Time to see exactly what Missy Charms is made of.
"What's up," she asked.

"I just got off the phone with Louis Reynolds."

"You're moving forward. That's good. Is he still with the Bureau?"

Nodding, he moved toward her, his intent unclear. "That's not what I want to talk about."

She waited, a sense of dread churning in her stomach.

"He had a lot to say about the funeral. *My* funeral."

At that she stood and prepared herself.

"He claimed you were pretty choked up. Especially for a widow who'd been planning a divorce."

She moved away, turning her back on him. "That was a very strange time for me, full of all kinds of conflicting emotions."

"I want to know, Missy." He was right behind her, his breath on her neck. "If you cared so much about me, then why were you divorcing me?"

"Why not? You were rarely around as I recall."

"Maybe there was a reason for that."

"Like what?" She spun around, all the hurt and anger of those days filling her up as if it were yesterday and she was lonely and miserable and dealing with a miscarriage all on her own because her husband was too focused on work to give a damn. She'd lost more than a baby that day in the hospital. She'd lost all hope for her marriage.

The words to try and explain were on the tip of her tongue, but what would telling him solve? She already felt incredibly vulnerable around him. The only thing saving her was his animosity. Lose that, and she might just find herself back to square one, loving a man who didn't love her.

"You know it wasn't easy being married to a Camden," he bit out.

"What does that mean?"

"Trying to live up to your father's expectations. And yours. The more I tried to take care of you, the more you complained. Apparently, your dad wasn't the only one I wasn't good enough for."

"That's not fair. All I ever wanted was for you to be there for me." She pushed past him, but he followed.

"Then why file for a divorce?" Fury sparked in his eyes.

"The fact that you have absolutely no clue ought to be clue enough."

"Missy—"

"You were never around, Jonas! I'm not sure why you ever married me. You were married to your job long before I ever came around."

"Then why did *you* marry *me?*"

"Because I loved you! Because I thought once we were married, I'd be your priority."

He didn't say a word. For a long moment, they quietly faced each other. Suddenly, his features softened. "You were my priority, Missy. Always. Every day."

"You sure had a funny way of showing it," she whispered.

He backed up, as if he didn't trust himself to remain close to her, and turned away. "You have no idea what it's like to be without money," he replied softly. "Can you even imagine coming home and finding out that your father's lost his third job in as many weeks? To see your mother get sick and worry over paying the medical bills? To get kicked out of your apartment because your father couldn't pay the rent?" He turned back, glanced at her and then quickly looked away again.

"I know you've never respected your father, but I didn't know how bad it was."

"I was ashamed of him."

"He's your father."

"We were homeless for a time, Missy. You can't possibly imagine what it's like to not know where you're going to sleep the coming night."

No. She couldn't. She had absolutely no frame of reference, and she'd had no idea his pain over his issues with his father ran so deep. God help her, but she wanted to reach out and hold him. "Jonas, if I'd known… If you'd shared." She moved toward him.

In an instant, he shut down. As if closing a door on his soul, his features hardened, his eyes turned guarded. "I swore that would never happen to me. Get it? No matter what, I would always provide for my family."

She reached out. "But, Jonas—"

"Don't touch me, Missy." He pushed open the door. "I can guarantee you won't like where I'll take it from there."

JONAS LEFT THE GIFT SHOP AND, knowing he wouldn't be able to stomach going back to Missy's house, headed to the lake to walk quickly along the shoreline. In a short while, he'd left the village behind and found a narrow path through the thick woods. He came to the lighthouse Missy had walked to the other night, wandered out toward the water and made himself sit quietly on a large flat rock.

He could see why she liked this place. The water was calm, as black as ink, and seemed to go on forever. A soft, cool breeze hit his face. There wasn't a sound but the waves lapping softly against the rocks. *Breathe it in. Relax. Slow down, Jonas.* It wasn't going to happen. Probably never would.

He couldn't believe he'd dredged up those old memories of his father. He should have felt relieved to have shared an inkling of his past with Missy, but all he felt was vulnerable and weak. He'd exposed himself. With a few choice words, she could cut him to the quick.

She wouldn't, though. Not Missy.

Or would she? Who filed for a divorce?

He would never be able to forget being rocked to the core when she'd come to him with those legal papers. The one person in the world he'd trusted had turned on him. And then cried at his funeral. Why?

Was it as simple as Missy claimed it to be? She'd felt lonely and unimportant? For the first time since she'd blindsided him with those legal documents Jonas realized that maybe he had given her cause. Maybe he was simply incapable of loving her back.

CHAPTER ELEVEN

"HAVE YOU FOUND HER?" Mason glanced again at the last known photo of the woman on his computer. She was attractive, in a refined, elegant sort of way, and he sure as hell couldn't picture her with the likes of Jonas Abel. Not back all those years ago when he went to her house to tell her Abel was dead and sure as hell not now.

"This isn't as easy as you'd think. She's changed her name so many damned times her trail is like a maze. Moved at least six times since Abel's death."

"She doesn't want to be found. Why?"

"You got me."

"Criminal past?" Mason mused. "A stalker or abusive boyfriend in her background? Nutcase?"

"None of the above as far as I can tell."

"I'll talk to Abel's old friends. Maybe they have something on her."

"What if Abel's wife is a dead end?"

"He's got to be with her. He couldn't have stayed under our radar all this time."

"Delgado's due back in Chicago any day. He's going to want this locked up."

Mason stood from his desk and glanced out onto the street. "So tell him what he wants to hear. That'll buy us a little more time."

"ENOUGH'S ENOUGH." SARAH CAME marching into Whimsy's back storage room. "You've been avoiding me and I want to know why."

Missy glanced up from the boxes she'd opened trying to find a new supply of recycled fabric purses from Thailand that had been practically flying off the shelves. One look at Sarah's face and Missy's stomach pitched. It'd been almost a week since she'd seen Sarah at Duffy's for happy hour.

Sarah put her hands on her hips. "I was going to wait until you were ready to talk, but I've had it."

"I haven't been—"

"Don't even try it," Sarah said, scowling. "I'm not Ron and you don't have me wrapped around your little finger. I want to know what's going on."

The comment about Ron was entirely uncalled for, but Missy couldn't fault Sarah for being upset.

"I'm sorry," Sarah said. "That was a low blow. I'm just worried about you. You haven't been yourself these last couple of days."

"Honestly, Sarah, I don't know where to begin."

"Anywhere is a start."

She was right. Enough was enough. Either Sarah was going to accept Missy for who she was, or not. Missy sat on a box. "I lied to you."

"About what?"

"Everything."

Sarah didn't say anything, only lowered herself onto another box and held Missy's gaze.

"Jonas isn't my brother."

Sarah chuckled and crossed her legs. "For some reason that doesn't really shock me."

"Wait a few minutes. It'll get more interesting." Missy took a deep breath. "He's my husband."

Sarah's eyes narrowed. "I thought you said your husband had died." Her voice betrayed her deep concern for Missy. That was bound to change.

Missy forged ahead, explaining everything she knew about Jonas's plan, knowing, at the very least, that Sarah wouldn't put Jonas at risk. "He truly thought he was making things easier for us both."

"He's an idiot."

"I'd filed for a divorce."

"Whoa."

Missy hesitated. "Everything happened so fast between us. I wasn't prepared for the realities of a relationship and he…he… An FBI agent's job is demanding. I felt so alone, even more so than before I'd met him. I'd started thinking we'd made a mistake. Then I got pregnant. I tried again to make our marriage work, but I miscarried the baby. He was out of town, unreachable, and I had to go to the hospital alone."

"You miscarried and went through it all by yourself?" Sarah seemed to fall back into her own past. As a single mother, she was sure to have gone through many things alone with her son though she'd never shared anything with Missy about Brian's father. The fact that they both seemed content sharing the present had been one of the things that had bound them as friends. "No wonder this adoption has been so important to you."

"I wanted that baby. If he'd been there, if I'd even been able to get ahold of him on the phone, maybe things would've been different. The fact that I couldn't talk to him at the most difficult time in my life was a last straw for me."

"You never told him that happened, did you?"

"At first it was all too raw. I was angry. Filed for a divorce almost right away. Not long after that he faked his death."

Sarah sighed. "Does he know the truth now? About the miscarriage?"

"No. I don't plan on telling him." The last thing she needed was to expose more tender spots to Jonas. Not after all that had happened between them.

"I'm not sure that's such a good idea, but you have to do what you think is right." Sarah put her arms around Missy and hugged her, but Missy shrugged away. In another minute or two, the only best friend Missy had ever had was bound to feel betrayed.

Sarah sat back. "There's more, isn't there?"

Missy nodded. The rest was the hardest part, but there was no going back. She'd started a ball rolling and she needed to follow through. Still, she couldn't look at Sarah, couldn't handle the pain of betrayal she was bound to see. "My real name isn't Missy Charms. It's Melissa Victoria Camden. I'm Arthur Camden's daughter."

"*Senator* Arthur Camden? Of the east coast Camdens? The famous family?"

Missy nodded.

As if she couldn't quite believe it, Sarah tried one more time. "You mean the Camdens who get mentioned on the entertainment channels? Whose pictures are on magazines and in newspapers?"

She nodded again.

"That means…that means you were once upon a time one of the richest children in United States history?"

Missy held her breath. *Please understand. Please.*

"Shit," Sarah muttered. "You're the daughter they never talk about. The one who's estranged from the family." She paused, seemed to be absorbing the information. "That's a damned big lie. Why?"

Missy tried to explain how she'd never felt a part of her family, how the fact that she'd had money—a lot of it—had changed how people looked at her, how she'd wanted to be someone other than who she was. "All my life. I just wanted to be normal."

"Normal? Like shop at second-hand stores normal? Like not sure how you're going to put food on the table normal? This is unreal." Sarah jumped up and paced what little she could amidst the boxes scattered across the floor. "So the other day when I told you about getting stiffed on that bill for that extravagant wedding and not being able to make my rent that month, you could've snapped your fingers and made the whole problem go away."

"I don't do that," Missy whispered. "Other than taking small amounts out for living expenses, I don't touch the money in my trust fund unless it's a crisis."

Sarah laughed sourly and shook her head. "And your best friend's crisis isn't your crisis?"

"That's not true. I knew you'd be okay, Sarah. I knew Ron, Jan and Marty would cut you slack."

"So what if the crisis had been worse? What if I was about to lose my house or my business? What then, Missy?"

She looked away, unable to bear the look of betrayal in Sarah's eyes. "I would've found a way to help, but probably wouldn't have told you about my family."

"Probably?"

"Sarah, you're strong. A helluva lot stronger than me. It's best for people to stand on their own two feet."

"Like you?" She shook her head. "Now I know how you can manage with a gift shop that never makes any money."

That stung. "I guess I deserved that."

"Does anyone else know about this?" Sarah asked.

"I told Ron and Jan the other day."

"What did they say?"

"Actually, they were relieved. They thought I was running from the police." She chuckled.

Sarah didn't even crack a smile. "Here I can't seem to get my head above water financially, and you have enough money to buy this entire damned island."

"I don't want to buy the island. I just want to be me."

"That begs the question…who exactly are you?"

Missy turned toward her, held her gaze. "You know who I am, Sarah. That, at least, hasn't been a lie. I am Missy Charms." She tried like hell to believe it.

"You're sure about that? Any other lies I should know about?"

Missy shook her head. "Sarah—"

Sarah went to the back door. "I have to go—"

"Can I tell you something first?"

Sarah crossed her arms in front of her, but at least she didn't walk away.

"I had a best friend in college," Missy started. "The first one ever, really. Chrissy was on scholarship and never had much spending money. She didn't come from a wealthy family. I think that's why I liked her so much. She was real, seemingly unaffected. Until she found out I was a Camden.

"The changes in our relationship didn't happen overnight, but before I knew it, she asked to borrow some money to pay for a movie. Promised to pay me back as soon as she got her next paycheck. She didn't, but I honestly didn't care.

"We'd go out shopping. She'd try things on, and then say she couldn't afford them. I'd feel bad and buy them for her. Little things like that kept happening.

"The real problems started when my mother invited her to come with us to France for spring break. My family paid for everything. Her airfare. All of her food and activities. They even took her on a shopping excursion and spent thousands on clothes for her.

"After that, nothing was ever the same between us. She'd borrow things from me and never return them, use my makeup, and stopped offering to pitch in on things. My CDs and DVDs would end up in her room. It didn't take long to start wondering why she wanted to be my friend."

Sarah said nothing.

"Chrissy wasn't the only one," Missy said. "I could go on and on about how the last name Camden impacted my relationships. Your friendship, Sarah, was too important to risk."

Sarah's eyes watered, but her expression remained resolute. "I have to think about this." She turned. "I'll get back to you."

As Missy watched her best friend walk away, what little was left of her world seemed to turn to dust at her feet. That had definitely not gone the way she'd hoped, but she couldn't blame Sarah if she never did get back to her.

Missy swiped her eyes dry, and oddly enough wished Jonas were here so she could talk. He'd always been such a good listener.

After letting Gaia know she was heading out for some air, Missy left Whimsy and took off down the street. She passed the small lot filled with Ron's equipment rental inventory, including strollers, bicycles and bike trailers meant to carry small children, as well as more active rentals like kayaks and windsurfing boards. Slowly, she stepped into Ron's shop, guessing she'd find Jan there, as well. It was very early in the afternoon and they usually made it a point to take lunch together.

Ron glanced up from helping a customer at the counter. "Well, I was wondering where you've—" He stopped and narrowed his eyes at her.

Jan hopped up from the table where she'd been eating a sandwich. "Missy, what happened?"

"I'm okay," she said. "I've just been crying."

"We can see that," Jan said, putting an arm around her shoulder.

"Let's go out back." Ron turned the customer he was helping over to one of his assistants and then drew Missy through the back workroom and out the door to the alley. Jan followed close behind.

Missy paced beside them. "I told Sarah the truth. All of it."

"Let me guess," Jan said. "She didn't take it very well."

Missy shook her head. "She was downright mad at me."

"I have to admit," Jan said. "At first, it hurt a little bit that you didn't trust us with the truth months, if not years, ago."

"I'm sorry." Missy glanced from one to the other. "There didn't seem to be any reason to bring it all up."

"Give her some time," Ron said, rubbing Missy's arm. "She'll realize that none of these revelations changes who you are deep inside, honey."

With that, Missy fell into his arms, big, strong arms that felt as if they could fight off the world. He rocked her back and forth as she cried. While her own father had done nothing except dictate, Ron had listened, counseled and consoled on more occasions than Missy could count.

Although it was possible Sarah might never forgive Missy, it'd been the right thing to do. Still, facing her and being honest with her had been one of the hardest things Missy had ever done. "I don't know what I'd do without you." She glanced at Jan. "You two have been more like parents to me in the last couple of years, than my real parents were in twenty."

"Some people just don't have it in them, Missy," Ron said, setting her away from him. "Then there are others we judge a bit too harshly."

She glanced at him. "You think I've been too harsh with my family?"

"No," he said. "I only wonder."

"I've never been a mother," Jan said, "but I imagine it must be hard for a woman to know her child has turned away from her, and I'm not sure blaming your siblings is fair. They were in the same boat with you, right?"

That's something Missy had never considered. "You're right. As usual." Missy sighed.

"What are you planning to do about Jonas?" Jan asked.

Another tough one, considering Ron and Jan's conservative views about marriage. "I know you don't believe in divorce, but there doesn't seem to be any other option."

"There are always other options," Jan said.

"He doesn't love me enough, and he loves his job too much." At least that's what Missy had been telling herself since Jonas first showed up on her porch, but after his admission the other day in Whimsy about the financial difficulties of his childhood, Missy was no longer sure about anything.

"Did you love him?" Ron asked.

Of that, there'd never been any doubt. "Yes."

"Well, then, seems pretty simple to me," Ron said. "Jonas

has been dead to you for four years, Missy. Things may have changed. Maybe you should give yourself more than a couple of days to decide what's for the best."

JONAS PACED MISSY'S HOUSE. Nearly every hour, he'd checked the e-mail account Louis Reynolds would be contacting and had found no messages. He should be doing something to get off this damned island. But what? He couldn't go back to Chicago and risk being discovered. He couldn't go to D.C. to face Stein and risk the investigation. There was still a chance they could bust Delgado. Hell, he couldn't even leave Missy's house. Every hotel room on the island was booked through the summer.

Missy.

Ever since he'd shared the truth about his childhood, he'd felt raw, like one big bullet wound. Now he was the one avoiding her. Memories of her, old and new, flooded in, and his anger, at her and himself, built. *Dammit!* He wanted to punch his fist through the wall. He should've never come here. Never. He'd thought he'd be safe with her. If only for a few weeks. His body might be healing, but it felt as if his heart was breaking all over again.

But that couldn't be. His heart wasn't—couldn't be—involved in this. He wouldn't let it come to that.

Work. That would distract him. There had to be something he could do. Keeping his fingers crossed that Reynolds had made some headway, Jonas dialed the agent's cell phone.

"Special Agent Reynolds."

"It's Abel. What do you know?"

"I'll make this quick. It appears your undercover op with Stein is not entirely legit."

"What does that mean?"

"It means Paul Kensington was so disgusted with the lack of progress on this assignment that he was about to shut you, Matthews and Stein down."

"That's bullshit! I've been filing weekly reports since this whole thing started." With the Bureau's attention turning away from drug trafficking and toward counter-terrorism since 9/11, the fact that things had fallen through the cracks on this case didn't surprise Jonas. That could mean only one thing.

"It looks like this thing is dead. Kensington wants you to come in."

"No." Jonas squeezed his eyes shut, trying to make sense of this. "Either Stein or Kensington, maybe both, are dirty."

"It's not Kensington. He's got too much to lose. Word is he might be up for director in a couple of years. Stein, on the other hand, just went through a nasty divorce."

Reynolds was only confirming what Jonas knew in his gut. "I'm not letting this go. I've got enough evidence here to bust this operation wide-open."

Reynolds said nothing.

"Don't you get it? Someone was using me and Matthews to gather evidence. Now they're going to sell it to Delgado."

"That's possible," Reynolds said, but there was something else. The concern in his voice was unmistakable.

"What's going on, Louis? What else did you find?"

"A half a million dollars wired into an offshore account. In your name."

"Son of a bitch." Jonas ran his hand through his hair. Most likely they were trying to discredit Jonas in order to buy some time. Why? What if Delgado's deal was still on?

But where? When? "If this was my baby why would I call you? They're setting me up."

"That was my guess, too, but Kensington isn't convinced."

"You already briefed Kensington?"

"I had to, Jonas. This is too big. Turns out he already had his eye on Stein."

Jonas had had enough of sitting around picking lint out of his belly button. Time to put this to bed. "I'm going after Stein."

"No, Jonas. That's an order from above. You are to remain where you are. Stay put. Let us work it out from this end."

"I can't do that."

"You don't have a choice. If you're going to do anything at all, send in the evidence you've accumulated these past two years on this drug cartel. Prove to everyone you're clean."

Jonas mulled that possibility over. It would take Reynolds some time to put all this evidence together for the appropriate warrants, but this was the only hope Jonas had of busting Delgado. And Stein. "All right. I'll overnight my files to you. Louis, be very careful."

The moment Jonas hung up the phone he copied every piece of data from his memory stick onto another one. Then he went to the village and mailed off all his files to Reynolds with a prayer that sacrificing the past four years of his life hadn't been for nothing.

He went outside, breathed in a lungful of fresh air, trying to clear his thoughts. It wasn't enough. Needing to be amidst people, even if they were strangers, he walked through town and ended up in front of the marina watching a charter boat returning. Excited tourists hopped onto the dock and posed for pictures with their catches of salmon and lake trout. They were joking around and generally enjoying their vacations.

Some guys had all the luck. He spun away from them and walked farther down Main. The sound of laughter and the smell of homemade fudge permeated the air as Reynolds's words echoed in his mind.

Your undercover op with Stein is not entirely legit.

He'd been living a damned lie in more ways than one and had given up on Missy all those years ago for no good reason. What was a man supposed to believe in?

He ran his hands over his face and caught his reflection in the front windows of Duffy's Pub. He'd lost everything he'd ever valued for this job and where had it gotten him? And where the hell did he go from here?

The old-fashioned red, white and blue pole outside the barbershop on the side street caught his eye. Immediately, he headed toward it. He could start by putting himself right again.

CHAPTER TWELVE

MISSY GLANCED UP AS TWO WOMEN came into her shop. The older one looked familiar—

Her adoption agent. "Barbara!" Missy skirted around the counter. "This is a surprise. I thought you were supposed to call me and I would come to Duluth. What in the world brings you to Mirabelle?"

"Missy, I know this is quite out of the ordinary," Barbara said, looking more than a little sheepish. "I apologize for not giving you notice, but this is the way Jessica wanted to meet you. Out of the blue. In your element, if you will."

Tell her. Tell her the truth about Jonas right now. There's no point in drawing this out.

The explanation formed in Missy's brain, but the words wouldn't come. As she glanced into the eyes of the clearly pregnant woman who'd come in with Barbara all thoughts of the truth flew her mind. An instant connection seemed to form between her and both the young woman and her unborn baby. This was meant to be. Missy could feel it as sure as she could feel her own heart beat.

"Missy, this is Jessica. Jessica this is Missy Charms."

"Hi," Jessica said.

"Hello, Jessica. Welcome to Mirabelle." Missy ached inside at the uncertainty she saw in those blue eyes. Nothing less than fate had brought her to Missy, but why? It didn't make sense. This adoption was bound to fall apart as soon as she told Barbara the truth about Jonas.

"So this is your gift shop, huh?" Jessica glanced around.

"This is Whimsy. Walk around, if you want."

Jessica took her time checking out one aisle after another. Missy gauged she couldn't be older than sixteen. With waist-length, straight brown hair and a loose-fitting peasant-type blouse, she looked like a throwback to the 1960s. Only the tiny gemstone piercing her nostril and the tattoo on her neck indicated she was a twenty-first century teen.

Barbara leaned toward Missy and whispered, "Normally, I wouldn't accommodate Jessica's request to visit unannounced, but she was insistent. I knew you'd do whatever it might take. Was I wrong?"

"No, you were right," Missy whispered back. "Jessica has every right to be careful. And I will do whatever it takes." She hadn't yet copped to Jonas's existence, had she? Even now, the lie weighed heavily on her mind.

"She's asked about your financial situation." Barbara continued to whisper. "But all we've told her is that you own your own home and business."

"I appreciate that," Missy said.

Jessica poked her head out from the end of an aisle. "What's fair trade?"

Missy explained that the profits from the merchandise she purchased went directly into the hands of the makers of the goods, rather than through intermediary wholesalers. "Cutting out the middleman helps a lot of mothers in poorer countries."

"Tight." She studied Missy.

Missy held her searching gaze. It was all she could do

not to reach out and place her hand on Jessica's bulging stomach. How amazing it must be to feel a baby growing inside, to feel her come to life, kicking, or hiccupping. Though she understood Jessica's decision, she imagined there were a few conflicting emotions going on inside the young woman.

Suddenly, back from her lunch break, Gaia burst into the shop. "Hey, Missy! Brought you back some pasta."

"Thank you." Missy took the take-out container. "Gaia, this is Jessica and Barbara."

Gaia's eyes widened. She'd worked for Missy long enough to recognize the name of her adoption representative.

"Hi." Jessica studied Gaia, took in her dreadlocks and the tiny hoops, but exactly what she was thinking wasn't immediately apparent. "Do you work for Missy?"

"My third summer." Gaia nodded.

"So you like working here?" Barbara asked.

"Like?" Gaia chuckled. "Missy's the best boss ever. I'm not sure I want to move on after college."

"Gaia, there's no need to embellish," Missy said, feeling uncomfortable.

"Well, it's true."

Suddenly embarrassed, Missy asked, "Would you like to go somewhere we can talk, get something to eat?"

"I think that's a good idea," Barbara said.

"I've got the store covered," Gaia announced with a smile.

Missy nervously stepped out onto the sidewalk. "There's a café by the marina that has wonderful salads."

"Can we see your house first?" Jessica asked.

Missy's heart felt as though it'd skipped a beat. If Jonas was in her home, this meeting would fall apart in seconds. She glanced at Barbara hoping the woman would give her an out, but the older woman only shrugged. There was no way out.

"Sure. Let's go." Missy led the way up the hill, saying one prayer after another.

"You didn't grow up here, right?" Jessica asked as they walked.

"I was raised out east. Long Island." By the time they'd reached her stone fence, she'd answered several more simple informational type questions. "Here we are."

Jessica glanced up and smiled. "This is your house? It's so pretty."

"Thanks." Missy was rather partial to it, as well. She unlocked the front door and breathed a sigh of relief that Jonas didn't appear to be around. Clutter was everywhere, as usual, but at least the place was relatively clean. "I'm sorry things are kind of cluttered."

She picked up a stack of mail on the counter and put it on top of her desk by the phone. Grabbed a couple of dishes and put them in the sink.

"Don't, Missy," Jessica said. "This doesn't look any messier than my own bedroom. You have a home. Not just a house." She walked around, taking in pictures and photos, the titles of books in her bookshelf.

"This is about it. My bedroom's in back."

Jessica went toward the hall. "Do you mind?"

"Not at all."

Barbara patted her shoulder. "You're doing great."

"Can I go upstairs?" Jessica asked.

"Um…it's…" Missy hesitated.

"Well, maybe it's time to get something to eat," Barbara said, coming to Missy's rescue. "We can visit better if we're sitting at a table."

Jessica looked around as if she wasn't yet ready to go, as if she might be trying to imagine how a baby might fit into the mix. Where would the highchair go? The crib? The toys? Would a baby living in this home be loved and cherished?

Yes, Missy's heart whispered. *Oh, yes.* "You ready, Jessica?" she asked, feeling suddenly overwhelmed by emotion.

"I think so." She turned and smiled at Missy. "Please call me Jessie."

A SHORT WHILE LATER, Missy waved goodbye to Barbara and Jessie as their ferry left Mirabelle's pier and motored smoothly toward Bayfield. The moment she lost sight of them, she dropped her hand and a sense of near desperation ran through her. Instead of finding resolutions, her life seemed to be getting more and more complicated.

She turned away from the pier and took off down Main, passing Duffy's. She'd missed happy hour this week for the first time in months, but she didn't yet have the courage to face Sarah. As she glanced up the block, her gaze immediately locked on a clean-cut man coming out of the barbershop. He was too far away to get a good glimpse of his face, but there was something familiar about his purposeful walk. The way he held his head, so straight and proud, his shoulders, broad and strong. The way his gaze seemed to pick up everything while pretending to notice nothing.

My God, it's Jonas.

He'd not only had his long hair buzzed off, he'd gotten every single whisker shaved off his cheeks and chin. As she moved closer Missy lost her breath. Those lips. Without the stubble on his cheeks, the lush fullness of his mouth became immediately apparent. Aside from the graying at his temples that was now visible with the shorter cut, this looked like the Jonas she'd fallen in love with. The Jonas who had broken her heart.

He noticed her immediately, and his eyes narrowed. "Missy."

"You shaved. Cut your hair. You look…"

"The way you remember me?" She would've expected for him to express some form of triumph, especially after the way she'd melted in his arms the other night, but the tone of his voice was as unreadable as ever. "I've always detested that long hair and beard," he explained. "Besides, my cover was blown."

She couldn't take her eyes off his face. "What are you doing downtown?"

"I called Reynolds. I needed to get out of your house."

"And?"

"It's getting messy. Now I'm being framed."

That didn't sound good, and while part of her wanted to dig into the details she wouldn't let herself get drawn in to his life. There was only one part of this new development that impacted her. "So you still can't leave Mirabelle?"

"Not yet." His gaze, holding a hint of regret, lingered on her face for a moment, and for a moment Missy spotted the old Jonas hidden deep under this man's protective layers. This man standing before her didn't merely look like the old Jonas. The old Jonas was truly there, under his skin.

God help her, but she wanted to touch his smooth face, urge that old Jonas to resurface. *We could start over. You and me. Adopt Jessie's baby and build a family, a life, here on Mirabelle. Maybe this time it would work.*

And maybe this time her heart would not only break, it

would shatter into a million pieces. Instinctively, she reached for the crystals around her neck and found instead the Chinese coin pendant Sarah had given her for her last birthday.

She was on her own.

"I WANT YOU TO DO SOMETHING for me," Delgado said.

Mason closed the door and, cell phone in hand, paced in his office. "What?"

"I have some packages delayed in customs. I have no doubt you could streamline the process."

"That's not part of our deal."

"It is now."

Now that Abel was causing trouble. "I'll see what I can do."

"Good. I will have someone call you later tonight with the details."

The moment his cell line went dead, Mason's office phone rang. The display showed the reception area, and he put the call on speaker. "Yes?"

"Senator Arthur Camden is here to see you."

What the…? Mason sat at his desk. The chair of the Senate Judiciary Committee wanted to see him. Why? This couldn't be good. "Tell him I'm out of the office. Tell him I'll call—"

"He's already headed—"

Mason's office door burst open and Senator Camden, dressed impeccably in a black designer suit, heavily starched white shirt and striped blue tie stepped into his office. "We were briefed yesterday on your fiasco in Chicago."

Mason hung up the phone and came around his desk. "I'm not sure I'd call it a fiasco—"

"What would you call one undercover agent confirmed

dead and the other taking bribes?" The senator paced. "A tea party?"

"Sir, I—"

"Have you found Abel?"

"Not yet, but we're working on it."

"What makes you think he's turned?"

"He took all the evidence with him and he hasn't called in. I'd say the writing is on the wall."

"Has he left the country?"

"We don't believe so."

"I have a personal interest in this case." Camden walked to the window looking out over Pennsylvania Avenue. "Jonas Abel is married to my daughter."

Holy shit.

"Melissa is estranged from the family and my wife would very much like to find her." He spun around and leveled his gaze at Mason. "The very second you locate Special Agent Abel, I want to be informed."

"Yes, sir."

The senator stalked out of Mason's office as quickly as he'd come. Mason shut the door and immediately dialed a number on his phone. "You're not going to believe this."

"I don't want to play guessing games with you, Mason."

"Her last name's Camden. As in the Long Island Camdens." Stein transferred the phone to his other ear. "As in Senator Arthur Camden's daughter."

"I know."

"What do you mean, you know?"

"I figured it out when I pulled their marriage certificate to find her maiden name and social. She's the one who cut off all ties with the family."

"That explains the name changes, the moves," Stein said. "Have you tracked her down?"

"Not yet. Without a legitimate warrant, I can't track any of the financial info. And the usual underground sources got nothing on her. Her attorneys have roadblocks up in every direction. It hasn't helped that she pretty much zig-zagged cross-country and then backtracked. I lost her in Milwaukee, but we're closing in on her."

"I'll see what I can do from my end."

"Don't worry. I'll have her nailed down in a day or two."

A FEW NIGHTS AFTER BARBARA and Jessie's surprise visit, Missy lay awake in bed staring at the ceiling and listening to Jonas calling out in his sleep. He'd had restless nights in the two weeks since he'd come to Mirabelle, but tonight was the worst. *"No sé. Para!"* he called out for the third time, and she debated what to do.

Although she'd been keeping the promise she'd made to herself by trying not to avoid Jonas, it hadn't been difficult. Jonas had been doing enough avoiding for them both. They'd made dinner together the past couple of nights, but the moment the last dish was washed, Jonas managed to find something to take him outside. While she caught up on a few things around the house, paying bills or balancing her checkbook, Jonas mowed the lawn. She did laundry. He pruned a couple trees. She changed the bed linens and he trimmed the bushes. Tonight, she'd been catching up on some Whimsy business when Jonas started scraping the chipping paint off her exterior window frames.

Not long after dark, she went to bed. A short while afterward, as if he'd been waiting for an all-clear, she'd heard Jonas come inside and head straight upstairs. Presumably, he'd fallen asleep, but he was not resting at all peacefully. A few hours later, she'd awoken to the sounds of him yelling.

"This is wrong," he called out. "Son of a bitch!" From English to Spanish and back again, his dialogue in his dreams bounced back and forth like a Ping-Pong ball. "Matthews, get down!"

Apparently, he was reliving the ambush where he'd gotten shot. He'd done this from time to time when they'd been married. While he was awake he'd analyze his cases, take them apart piece by piece to make sure he hadn't made any mistakes, to see where he could improve. Sleep only brought on another level of analysis.

Most often he'd only talked in his sleep, usually not more than a word or two, a sentence at most. A few times, he'd actually thrashed about, carrying on for long periods in this same type of frenzied, chaotic state.

Back then she'd tried everything to get him to quiet down. Waking him hadn't worked. As soon as he'd fallen back asleep, he'd start at it again. She'd tried earplugs and moving to another room. He'd been too loud. There'd been only one thing that had calmed him, only one thing had helped them both fall back to restful sleep. She'd snuggled against his backside. Only her touch had relaxed him.

Jonas groaned loudly. Quieted for a few minutes, though she could hear him tossing about, and then started up all over again.

She glanced at the clock. Two. She'd gotten, at best, a couple hours of sleep and had to be up and about in a little more than four hours, and Jonas had given no indication he'd settle down any time soon. She didn't have earplugs, and a pillow hadn't worked to block the noise. There was only one thing she could think to do. While it didn't sit well, it seemed her only option. Besides, she'd decided she'd no longer avoid him.

Throwing back the covers, she climbed the stairs and snuck quietly into Jonas's room. He was on his back, tossing his head back and forth and muttering to himself. The last thing she wanted to do was place her hands on his body. From the first to the last, every time she'd ever touched this man, her body had gone crazy with need. She was asking for trouble simply being in a bedroom with him, thinking this way, feeling this way.

Nonsense. You were only twenty-three when you met him. You had no self-control back then. Things can be different today.

She took a deep breath, slipped her hands under his covers and slowly placed her palms over the tops of his ankles. He was warm. She was warmer. The coarse hair on his legs tickled her fingers, sending a zap of awareness up her arms and she almost pulled away. In order for this to work, though, she had to clear her own mind.

He wields no more power over you. You are in complete control. You can help him, give to him, without losing a piece of yourself.

Closing her eyes, she relaxed her arms, let her hands lay heavy on his ankles and focused on calming him. Once he relaxed, she could possibly find and clear his energy, helping him heal, helping him rest.

Jonas. Settle. Find the peace in your heart.

ONE GUN SHOT. TWO.

Jonas ran through the empty parking ramp. They were almost on him, two steps behind him. Suddenly the only footsteps he heard were his own.

Watching. They had to be watching, but who were *they?* What were they waiting for? He could feel their eyes on him. Behind him. Over him. Almost as if they were inside him.

Out of breath, he stopped and yelled, "Who the hell are you?" Then he spun around and fired several rounds into the air, at nothing and everything at once. He paused to listen and catch his breath.

Suddenly, as if he'd stepped into a hot pool, warmth enveloped his ankles. The warmest touch he'd ever known. Gently. Softly. Hands held him. Deep, bone-melting heat traveled up his legs. Suffused him with a sense of calm. As if he'd become a slow, lazy river, his breathing slowed.

How could this be? He never—

Missy. She was touching him. It had to be her. Jonas hovered between the states of sleep and awareness. Half of him felt almost tormented by the knowledge she'd place her hands on him. The other half desired nothing less than to sink into the oblivion of her sweet touch.

Infinitely slowly, with the kind of patience Jonas never had, never would possess, her hands moved over him. Her heat transmitted deep into the marrow of his bones, and a sense of relaxation like nothing he'd ever felt wrapped Jonas in a cocoon. She moved from his ankles to his knees. Then to his hips and ribs. All over him at once as if she had eight arms.

"What are you doing?" he whispered before he felt sure he'd relax to the point of losing all ability to speak.

She pulled away. "I thought you were asleep."

"I was, but don't stop." He kept his eyes firmly closed. "Please."

Hesitantly, her fingers rested on his forehead, hot and heavy on his cool skin. "It's called Healing Touch. Clears and balances your energy. Helps you heal faster."

"Chakras shit?" he murmured.

"Yes."

"When did you learn to do this?" he asked, almost slurring his words.

"Over the years." Her touch grew stronger, more assured. "It's been an interest of mine."

Didn't surprise him. Her hands always had worked magic on him. Lots of magic. His thoughts tracked to the other night and all he could think of was how she'd come alive in his arms. Her hands moved to his chest and his pulse raced. His mouth turned dry. He couldn't swallow.

That's when he felt it, the subtle change in sensation. Her fingertips curled into him, her nails nearly bit into his skin. Suddenly there was nothing healing about her touch. This was an outright jolt of raw, sexual heat, coursing through him like a drug.

No. Not again. He grabbed her wrist and snapped open his eyes. "I'm going to guess my chakras are just fine now."

Her eyes were heavy-lidded. Her breath came in short pants. She pulled against his grip on her wrists.

"Tell me something," he murmured.

She stared at him, distrust sparking in her eyes.

"That night we met at that bar in Quantico, what did you see in my hands?"

For a long moment, she said nothing. He'd almost given up on an answer when she whispered, "Your love line. Looks exactly like mine. One true love in your life."

"That's bullshit. There's no such thing as love, Missy. We had sex. Great sex. Amazing sex. But still just sex. It's not the kind of thing real people build lasting relationships around."

"If you say so."

He didn't just say so. He knew so. They'd failed, hadn't they? "Then why file for a divorce? Sounds like a damned easy way out to me."

"Staging your death wasn't?"

He released her and looked away. "I need to get back to sleep."

"You do that, Jonas," she said, heading toward the door, "While you're at it, keep telling yourself that our marriage failing was entirely my fault."

No, he wasn't fool enough to tell himself that. Not anymore. "Missy?"

She paused on her way out of the room.

For a moment, he couldn't speak. Emotions seemed to overwhelm him. "Thank you," he whispered. "For the... healing massage." As she went back downstairs, he knew there'd be no more nightmares tonight because he wouldn't be falling back to sleep.

CHAPTER THIRTEEN

EVERYTHING SEEMED WRONG.

Chin in hand, Missy sat at the front counter and contemplated her shop. Her thoughts felt disjointed and scattered. It had to be due to how the shelving in her store was arranged. The energy couldn't flow. Even her thoughts were all over the place. One minute she worried about Sarah. The next about Jessie and her baby. More often than not, her thoughts had something to do with Jonas.

What had she been thinking last night? Putting her hands all over him? Healing touch or not, she'd been out of line. Delirious from lack of sleep. That had to be it. But he'd sure felt good. Amazing contradictions of hard and soft, hairy and smooth. Warm. No. Hot.

She sucked in a quick breath and tried to eradicate from her mind the remembered image of his hand on her wrist. She'd always loved his fingers, the way his dark hair traveled up the back of his hand. Damn. Then again, her problems most likely had nothing to do with blockage of energy. Her entire life was a mess. Jonas. Sarah. Her family.

Marin. A long forgotten memory about her sister poked at Missy. Throughout much of their elementary years, Marin, despite the fact that she was older, often crept quietly into bed with Missy on Sunday nights. Missy had never said a word. Her sister hated going to their strict private school, and Mondays were the worst. Missy smiled, sadly, wondering if her sister still dreaded Monday mornings, or if she was happy in her job, her life.

It was time to tackle one more issue. Abruptly, she dialed a number she'd kept stored but unused on her cell phone all these years.

"Rutherford and Barker," a receptionist said, answering. Missy couldn't breathe.

"Hello? Anyone there?" the woman said.

"Um." She swallowed. "Is…Marin Camden in?"

"One moment, please."

Without any transfer noises, the sounds of soft classical music played over the line, letting Missy know she'd been placed on hold. She looked out her window, took a deep breath and made herself wait.

"This is Ms. Camden's office," said, most likely, a personal assistant. "She's in a meeting with clients at the moment, may I take a message?"

"This is Marin's sister, Melissa…Camden. Could you please—"

"Excuse me, did you say *sister? Melissa?*"

"Yes."

"Hold, please."

That was weird. The classical music came back online while Missy waited. And waited. Her hands may have finally stopped shaking, but now she was getting supremely irritated.

Suddenly the music clicked off and a long moment of silence hung on the line. Then, tentatively, a voice whispered, "Melissa?"

"Marin, is that you?"

"Holy freaking shit! It's really you."

Missy laughed. "Sounds like it's really you, too."

Marin was to Missy as night to day. Marin swore, sweat and walked around with a chip on her shoulder the size of a Lake Superior boulder. Missy never had found common ground with her sister, one of the few people on this earth with whom Missy should've been able to connect.

"I don't believe it," Marin said. "I don't even know what to say."

Neither did Missy it'd been so many years.

"Where are you?" Marin finally asked.

Missy hesitated. The one question she wasn't sure she wanted to answer, but she hadn't thought to block her number, so it wouldn't take much for someone as resourceful as a Camden to locate Missy. "Don't tell Dad, okay? I'm on Mirabelle Island, Wisconsin. I've been here for about two years."

"And this is the first time you bother to call and touch base?" Marin asked, the tone of her voice laced with a definite note of challenge if not hurt feelings.

"I guess I didn't think anyone would care—"

"Not care? You don't get it, do you?"

"I didn't ask to be born a Camden."

"Well, you were, so get over it. Do you have any idea how many tears Mom has shed over your immature and incredibly selfish disappearance? Maybe you should be calling her first. Maybe I just don't give a shit. Maybe…"

Missy didn't know what to say.

"You know, for the first couple of months after you disappeared, everyone pretended you'd show up. Eventually. Then the holidays rolled around and no phone call, no letter. Nothing to let any one of us know you were still even alive."

Missy probably *had* only thought of her side of this equation. "I'm sorry, Marin. Honestly, I never thought me disappearing would make a difference to you, Max or Art. Dad, I don't care about. And Mom? I guess I didn't want to think about her."

"Well, that sounds all very well and convenient. Good for you, Mel."

The use of the childhood nickname after all these years felt like a punch to the gut. Maybe she had been more connected to her siblings than she'd realized. "This was…difficult…to call you."

No sound. Nothing.

"Marin?"

"You know what? Maybe you being out of my life wasn't such a bad thing after all."

Click.

Her sister had hung up and Missy couldn't think of a reason why she had a right to feel the slightest bit indignant.

JONAS GLANCED AT HIS WATCH. His wound was healing as well as could be expected and he had most of his energy back, so he'd spent the majority of the day repairing Missy's stone fence along the front sidewalk. Now it was well past dinnertime, and he was starving.

He put away the tools and supplies in the shed in Missy's backyard, cleaned up and didn't bother scrounging around in the kitchen for something to eat. Lunch had proven he'd eaten through everything from his last run to the grocery store, so he walked into town for dinner and planned to stop at the grocery store afterward. By the time he finished a burger at the Bayside Café, the little village was on the verge of closing up. A trip down Main proved Newman's closed for the night, and he was heading back to Missy's house when he passed her gift shop.

It was the only store along the block, other than Duffy's, with lights beaming through the windows. It seemed odd Missy had chosen to stay this late, especially after the way she'd been making it a point to no longer avoid him. He couldn't shake the feeling that something was wrong.

Jonas opened the door to her store and stepped inside. The other night when he'd charged in here bent on verifying that Reynolds had been right about Missy falling apart at his funeral, he hadn't paid any attention to the surroundings. Today the place nearly overwhelmed him in its Missy-ness.

A sweet, fruity scent permeated the evening air. Music, if that's what you could call that new age instrumental sound, came softly from the direction of what he presumed was the front counter. Although there was no way to tell where purchases were to be made from browsing areas. The place was in complete and total disarray.

Merchandise lined the haphazardly arranged shelving units with no discernable rhyme or reason. Several shelves were in various stages of being dismantled and rearranged, stock was piled everywhere, and Missy was nowhere to be found.

"Missy, you here?" he called.

"Go away." She sounded so pathetically miserable he could barely keep himself from smiling.

Sidestepping a couple of boxes stacked in the middle of an aisle, he headed toward the sound of her voice. He found her sitting on the floor, her elbows resting on her knees, her head in her hands, and something in him softened to mush.

The expression on her face was exactly the one he remembered so many years ago when he'd come home to find her in their kitchen in the midst of making vegetable lasagna. From scratch. Fresh tomatoes were bubbling in too small a pan on the stove. Grated mozzarella was everywhere. Chunks of Romano had landed in her hair.

One look at her back then and he'd forgotten he was hungry. They'd made love on the kitchen floor amidst fresh crushed basil and slices of eggplant. What he wouldn't give to go back to that moment and start all over again. Maybe this time he could fix it before it all fell apart.

Right. And he was a calm, patient, loving man.

He looked away for a moment, gathered himself, and then asked, "What's going on?"

"Why would you care?"

He raised his eyebrows at her, and that's when he noticed she wasn't wearing the protective crystals around her neck.

"Oh, all right!" Her shoulders sagged. "I wasn't happy with the flow of energy in here. I was trying to feng shui the space and all I've done is messed up everything." She glanced at him. "Go ahead. Gloat."

She reached up to run a hand through the curls of her long hair and the tattoo markings on the inside of her left arm became visible, and gloating was the last thing on his mind. Obviously, due to the placement of the tattoos on the underside of her arm, they were important to Missy from a personal standpoint as opposed to trying to send a message to the world. Quickly, he stifled the urge to ask her what they meant.

"What is *feng shui,* anyway?"

She studied him for any crack in his sincerity. "Literally, it means wind-water," she said. "It's a way of arranging space and color to create harmony in life by keeping the positive energy flowing."

Who was he to judge? Whether feng shui worked or not,

Missy believed it did, and that's all that really mattered. "What were you trying to do?"

"Move this aisle over there and that one over here." She pointed this way and that as she explained her master plan.

"So where's the problem?"

"I can't move the shelves, Gaia's already gone home for the day, and this is a bigger job than I expected." She shrugged. "I'm all out of energy."

"You plan on opening in the morning, don't you?"

"Well, yes, b—"

"Then let's go. If anyone can do this it's you."

Distrust clouded her eyes. "Why do you say that?"

He wasn't exactly sure why he'd made that statement, but he knew it to be true.

"Jonas?"

"Because you're not only a dreamer, Miss," he finally answered. "You make dreams come true."

"You say that like it's a good thing."

"Where would this world be without dreamers? Without people who looked outside the box and took on new challenges?" For all his analytical pragmatism, Missy's outlook on the world was one of the things that had initially drawn him to her years ago and even now pulled him in.

She hesitated.

In spite of everything between them, he found himself holding his breath for her. *You can do it, Miss.* He held out his hand to help her stand. "You're stronger than you think. I'll help. So let's do this."

"Why? Why would you help me when you should walk away?"

"I've disturbed the feng shui of your life enough. The least I can do is make it up to you by helping feng shui your shop." Besides, he had nothing better to do while he sat tight waiting for Reynolds to get his files and work some magic with the Bureau. He might as well make himself useful.

She studied him for a moment as if deciding whether or not he was being honest, and then on a heavy sigh, reached up and put her hand in his. She was so light he easily pulled her to her feet.

"Okay, boss lady. Tell me what to do."

For the next hour, Missy told him where she wanted things moved and he moved them. Some things she'd gotten right the first time and other things had to be shifted around once or twice. When she'd settled on the placement of the main shelves and racks, they spent the next hour or so restocking.

Jonas did his best to stay in any aisle except for the one she was in. Being near Missy, smelling her, listening to her soft, calm voice was doing a number on him. At one point, she sent him into the back room for something. He took one look around at the mayhem in her storage area and knew exactly what he'd be doing the next day.

Even so, it was hard to fault Missy. What she lacked in organizational skills she more than made up for with heart. He hadn't been able to keep from noticing the origins of her inventory. Missy was helping a damn lot of people.

By the time he'd placed the last item, a set of earth-friendly stationery, on a display case his bullet wound, which had previously been healing quite nicely, was aching. Even so, Jonas stepped back, admired his handiwork and grinned. "I'm done. You have anything else that needs to be shelved?"

"Nope. We're finished." Missy popped up from another aisle, stood toward the back of the shop and a big smile spread across her face. "I like it. What do you think?"

What he liked was looking at her, the way her hair bounced, her smile widened, her eyes twinkled. He'd promised to not touch her, but touching her seemed the only thing on his mind. He went back to where she stood to get the same view. "It looks clean to me. Like I could easily move through the aisles without bumping into things."

"Exactly." She walked through the store grinning. "This is perfect. Perfect." She was perfect. She glanced at him, a ray of warm sunshine on a cold, bitter day. "Thanks for your help. I couldn't have done this without you."

"Yes, you could've. You would've."

"It definitely would've taken me all night."

"Probably."

"Let's go home," she said with a soft smile.

Home. What a damn loaded word.

"HUNGRY?" MISSY ASKED as they walked through her front door.

"Now that you mentioned it, I'm starving."

"Salad? Pasta?"

He hesitated. "I'm pretty hungry. Maybe I'll go back to town—"

"I have the makings for a homemade potpie."

He looked at her. "Vegetarian?"

She nodded. "But it's hearty. I promise you'll feel satisfied." At least your stomach will, she almost added and then thought better of it.

"What can I do to help?"

"Open that bottle of merlot and then help me chop some onions." She flipped on the oven and then gathered the ingredients. Onions and garlic. Peas, carrots and corn. Vegetable broth, bay leaves. Potatoes, barley, pie crusts.

He glanced skeptically at the bottle of merlot.

"You used to like wine." She started peeling a potato.

"Haven't had the occasion for it these last several years. The lot I've been forced to hang with are more of a tequila shot kind of group."

"If you'd prefer—"

"No, I wouldn't." He took out a corkscrew and opened the bottle. "I'm quite sure I'll never drink tequila again."

They stood next to each other at the counter, and Missy felt herself relaxing with Jonas for the first time since he'd reappeared in her life. It hadn't happened often, but years ago when Jonas had come home early from work they'd have invariably found themselves in the kitchen making a meal together. After all they'd been through it was nice to recapture a hint of the good times.

"Where did you live while you were undercover?" she asked.

"Apartment in Chicago. Wasn't in too bad a part of town, but it was nothing more than four walls, really. Sterile." He poured two glasses of wine and then downed the better part of one. "I couldn't have anything personal around that might give me away."

Missy couldn't imagine it. She almost reached out to pat his back. But if he couldn't touch her, she couldn't touch him. She sautéed the onions and garlic. "Wasn't there any part of the life that your were living that resembled your own?"

"No." He refilled his wineglass.

"Never dated? Went to movies? Checked out restaurants?"

"No. No. And no." He grabbed a knife and chopped vegetables. "I worked. Put together evidence. Filed reports. Listened to wiretap recordings. Deciphered e-mails."

She watched his face and remembered that look. "Bad men, huh?"

"Very." He sliced quickly, hitting the chopping block harder and harder with each thrust.

"Can you tell me about it?"

"I'm not sure you'd want to hear."

"I'd like to—"

"It was as bad as it gets, Miss." Pausing, he glanced at her. "We were holding out to nail Delgado. The top man. At least I thought that was the holdup. Anything you can imagine, I saw. Beatings. Murders. Teenage drug dealers and prostitutes. And much worse." He glanced out the window as if remembering. "No respect for life. Few lives worth respecting."

Through it all, one thing she'd never lost for Jonas was respect. What she did to help the unfortunate was nothing compared to what Jonas had accomplished as an FBI agent.

She shouldn't ask, she knew, but a part of her cared deeply about his work. "What's going to happen to this assignment?"

"I've worked too long and hard to let these last four years amount to nothing. I'll nail them all to the wall, if I can."

She took a gulp of wine, summoning the courage for a question that had been popping into her mind lately. "What if you couldn't…nail them? What if you could no longer be an FBI agent?"

"It's who I am, Missy," he whispered, going back to chopping vegetables. "I don't see that changing any time soon."

THE NEXT MORNING, MISSY WAS answering a customer's questions about fair trade products when sounds coming from the back room distracted her. She finished the sale of the coffee beans from South America and spun around expecting to find

Ron had come into her store from the alley. No doubt he'd had enough of the disarray in her storage room.

"Hey!" she said, smiling, and then stopped at the sight of a large, muscled body bent over clearing a space on the floor. "Jonas?"

"Morning."

Wanting to get to her shop early to make sure she was satisfied with the rearrangements, she'd left her house before he was awake. "What are you doing here?"

He grinned. "Feng shui-ing your back room."

"Awesome." Gaia showed up beside Missy. "This the guy who helped last night?"

"Jonas, this is Gaia. Gaia, this is…my husband, Jonas." On one level it felt so entirely strange to introduce him as her husband, and yet so normal on another.

"Legit." Gaia raised her eyebrows and nodded with approval.

"He won't be around for much longer," Missy added, trying to distance herself. "So there's no point in getting to know him."

"If you say so." Gaia spun around and went back into the store.

"You don't need to do this," Missy said as he pulled out one of the shelving units Ron had purchased months ago and began assembling it.

"I want to." Sidestepping boxes stacked every which way, Jonas came toward her. "If it makes you feel any better I'm bored out of my mind. I need to do something to pass the time."

Missy backed up as the overwhelming urge to walk toward him engulfed her. No man had ever made her feel quite this real, this free to be herself. His stable, no-

nonsense way of going through life had always calmed her thoughts, her energy. As long as he wasn't touching her, as long as they didn't make love, being near Jonas somehow grounded her.

The problem was all she wanted was to touch him.

"Thanks." She backed up even more. "I'll be out front if you need anything." Then she quickly escaped.

Unfortunately, nearly the entire day while Missy occupied herself with customers, her thoughts were actually focused on Jonas. She'd hear the sound of a drill and wonder how many shelves he'd assembled. A box would slide across the cement floor and she couldn't help but imagine how he may have arranged the shelving. Long moments of complete and total silence made her wonder what he was organizing.

By lunchtime she couldn't stand it. Needing to get away, she ran to the Bayside, brought back several sandwiches and asked Gaia to deliver a couple to Jonas. The afternoon was no different from the morning. It was early evening when he hesitantly came out front.

"Missy?"

She turned from rearranging the window display. "Need some help?"

"Actually, it's finished. Do you want to see? You might like to make some changes."

Missy followed him into the back room with Gaia hot on her trail.

"Owned!" Gaia said, walking around looking at the shelving. "This totally smokes."

Missy was speechless. She barely recognized the area. All the clothing was shelved on one unit, the home and garden merchandise on two others, and books, calendars, cards and all type of paper products on another. Apparently she had enough jewelry for one entire storage unit. Purses and wallets took up most of another.

"I can't believe this," she murmured. "I can actually walk around back here." There was even enough room for a small table and a couple of chairs for short breaks.

"Ron is going to be so happy," Gaia added. Then a customer came to the front counter with a purchase. "I'll get it."

"What do you think?" Jonas grinned at Missy. "Six weeks before you're going to need someone to get back in here and organize things?"

Her heart felt as if it stopped. "What if you were still here? Would that be so bad?"

Jonas's smile disappeared. "That's not going to happen, Missy."

Of course not. Missy took a deep breath and did her best to smile. "You know what? Gaia's closing the shop tonight, so let's go. I owe you dinner." She headed toward the front door. "How does Duffy's sound?"

"All right. You're on."

CHAPTER FOURTEEN

MISSY WALKED INTO DUFFY'S PUB and glanced through the windows in the main dining area that looked out over Lake Superior. Only a sliver of the sun clung to the horizon, shedding its pale light on the sailboats docked in the harbor and creating a quiet, romantic atmosphere. Not what she was after. Besides, Missy had always preferred the dark and somewhat raucous pub side. After nodding to a few of her fellow islanders, she took a seat in the first available booth not far from the bar.

Jonas sat directly across the table from her. Their waiter, a college kid, handed them a couple of menus. Missy didn't bother with hers. "Eggplant parmesan," she said, after ordering a glass of merlot.

Jonas flipped back and forth through the menu.

"Erica makes the most amazing pasta," she offered.

"Why don't you order for me?" Jonas handed the menu back to the kid.

"He'll take the rigatoni."

"And a beer."

The waiter walked away, quickly came back with their drinks and they sat looking at each other. This was getting dangerous. Spending the last night with him rearranging her gift shop and listening to him work his magic this morning in her back room had reminded her of the many reasons she'd fallen in love with the man.

"Why Mirabelle?" he asked, out of the blue. "I would've thought you'd go to L.A. or Seattle. New Mexico. The Midwest seems a little staid for you. How'd you end up here?"

It seemed too personal to share that she'd been looking for the right kind of place to raise a few kids. "I'm not really sure," she finally said. "I guess I hit the road right after you died. Had no idea where I was going. First stop was Sandusky, Ohio, along the shores of Lake Erie. Then Gary, Ludington and Traverse City along Lake Michigan. Then I took a long road trip through Montana, Wyoming, Oregon." At least that was the truth. She took a sip of wine, glanced at him over the rim of the glass, then set it down. "But you already know that, don't you?"

Silently, he nodded.

"Turned out I liked the Great Lakes best. So I headed back to the Midwest. Not sure why. Big water, I guess. Without the saltiness of the northeast coast."

"Wisconsin's a bit off the beaten path."

"I just drove, Jonas, letting my instincts lead me, until I hit water. This time the water in my way was Lake Superior. When I got to Bayfield, there was a ferry heading to Mirabelle. I got on it and never looked back." She smiled. "Besides, except for Manhattan, where else can you live and not own a gas-guzzling, global-warming-causing car?"

Jonas smiled. It was unusual to see him so relaxed she found herself staring. "What kept you here?" he asked. "On an island? You never stayed any other place longer than a few months."

"The people, I suppose." She sipped her wine. "They're straightforward. If they like you, you're in like Flynn. If they don't, they let you know. I can deal with that."

"Some of them didn't like you? Impossible."

"Mary Miller—she owns the candy shop—still looks the other way when I walk down the street. Shirley Gilbert, the owner of the cotton-candy-pink B and B, can be rude. Outright. Even Jan Setterberg wasn't the most hospitable of neighbors until I got to know her sister, Lynn Duffy, a little better."

"Doesn't make sense. How can anyone resist you?"

"You did."

"Is that what you think? That I was unaffected by you? That I ignored you?"

"It's not what I thought as much as what I felt."

He looked away, seemed angry. When he glanced back at her, he'd recovered, just barely. He glanced at her arm. "Tell me what those mean. Your tattoos."

She hesitated, unsure she cared to share something so intimate. Then again, what could be the harm? Jonas would be gone in a week, two at most. The thought made her feel fairly miserable.

"Missy? You okay?"

"They're the Sanskrit symbols for the chakras," she finally whispered. "The first one is the crown. Our spirituality. The next one, our third eye, represents intuition or wisdom. Then there's the throat."

"Let me guess." He smiled. "Communication."

She nodded. "Our self-expression."

He reached out to touch the fourth symbol and then, as if he remembered his promise to not touch her, quickly pulled back. "Next is the heart, isn't it?"

"Which needs no explanation," she said, almost wishing she hadn't held him to his promise. "Then the solar plexus. Which holds our personal power. The sacral chakra embodies our emotional balance and sexuality."

"That's odd," he whispered. "Those two going together."

"Is it?"

He gaze faltered for a moment. "Maybe not."

"And last is the root. Represents our survival. Our physical needs."

"So why those symbols and why there?"

She hesitated. "They remind me what's important to me. Help me remember who I am."

"I noticed you aren't wearing your crystals anymore."

"I need to protect myself without help," she said.

"And I have no doubt you can."

His eyes held her mesmerized. For a moment, she fought the connection growing between them, fearing the weakness she'd experienced all those years ago around Jonas. Fearing she might slip back in time and lose the ground she'd gained. But there was nothing weak or needy about what she felt toward Jonas. She felt strong, alive and whole. Though utterly confused.

The waiter came to their table, delivering food, and the moment evaporated as quickly as it had come. They were finishing eating when Sean came into the bar. Nodding at Missy, he came to their booth after picking up a beer at the bar. "Hey."

"Sit," Missy said, glad for the diversion. "Have a beer with us."

"Nah, I don't want to disturb your meal." He glanced at her, studied her face, and then, reconsidering, suddenly plopped down next to her. "On second thought maybe I will," he said, looking directly at Jonas. "Got a haircut, I see."

Jonas nodded, almost imperceptibly before taking his last bite of pasta. Tension charged between the two men like boxers squaring off in opposite corners.

"How's your side healing?" Sean asked, although there was no compassion in his voice.

"Fine."

"Great." Sean put his arm on the back of the booth behind Missy in a subtly possessive way. "So when are you leaving?"

Under the booth, Missy briefly put her hand on Sean's leg. *Don't. It's okay.*

"Actually, I'm kind of liking Mirabelle." Jonas took a long pull on his beer. "Maybe I'll stay awhile."

She could almost hear the vibrations coming off Jonas. *My wife, asshole. Hands off.*

"Won't the FBI be wanting their agent back?"

"I'm not sure I'll be staying with the Bureau." He held Sean's gaze for a moment and then briefly glanced at Missy.

What? That threw her. Jonas without the FBI was like tofu straight up. "What would you do?" she asked.

"I've heard Newman's grocery store is looking for a security guard," Sean said, sipping his beer.

Jonas glared at Sean and then ran a hand over his face and chuckled. "Or I suppose I could bounce here at Duffy's. Get rid of all the riffraff."

Missy glanced between the two men. "Okay, that's it. Far much too testosterone. I'm out of here." She pushed Sean out of the booth and then slid out behind him.

"I'll walk you home," Sean said.

"I think, at this point, I'd rather be alone."

AFTER MISSY LEFT DUFFY'S PUB, Sean slid back into the booth and leaned forward. "What do you want from Missy?"

Damned good question. One Jonas could not definitively answer. "I don't see how my relationship with my wife is any of your business."

"Wife. That's a good one."

"I don't need to explain myself to you," Jonas answered softly.

"No. I suppose you don't." The doctor shook his head. "I just can't seem to figure out what she saw in you."

That made two of them, but it didn't mean the comment went over well with Jonas. "For Missy's sake, I'm going to pretend you didn't say that."

Sitting back, he took a slow, measured breath and put the lid on his rising anger. He slapped a couple twenties on the table to cover their dinner and then some and stood. "Why don't you have another beer, Doc. On me."

BIRDS CHIRPED AND TRILLED outside the open window, robins, chickadees, sparrows and finches. A crow cawed in the distance. Jonas lay in bed and breathed in the clean, cool morning air blowing into his room. A little more than two weeks had passed since he'd first stepped foot on Mirabelle and already he felt more relaxed than he could ever remember. He could get used to this. The only thing that would make this morning even better was Missy snuggled in the crook of his arm.

Maybe in another life.

Then again, maybe never.

He eased himself out of bed and went downstairs. Missy was already gone, but after last night at Duffy's with Sean that was no surprise. Even before he made a pot of coffee,

Jonas logged onto the Web site where he was waiting for Reynolds to post a notice that he had further developments. There was one message with several attachments.

Call me. Secure line.

Jonas didn't recognize the number. He used a safe cell phone and dialed.

Reynolds picked up immediately. "That you?"

"Yep."

"Damn, man, you've got a lot of evidence here. Right after I briefed Kensington on how thorough you've been he assembled a team. They're working round the clock to put this together."

Jonas swallowed and relief swept through him. This is what he needed to hear. "What about Stein?"

"Business as usual. He has no clue we're on to him. Did you look at the files I sent?"

"What are they?" Jonas said, opening them.

"We tracked some of Stein's e-mails."

Jonas studied the documents. "He's clearing things through customs."

"That's what it looks like. We've got our best agents on this. They're clean. We might be ready to take down the whole organization in a few days."

"No," Jonas said. "We do that and we won't get Delgado. Wait. Trust me. He's personally handling this next deal. If you nail him with the goods in hand, you got him."

"When do you think it's going down?"

Jonas studied the details of Stein's e-mails, the dates, the number of packages and the weights. "I'll bet anything this happens in the next week."

"We need a time and a place."

"I'll figure it out." Jonas hung up the phone.

Easier said than done.

He made some coffee, found out cereal with soymilk wasn't actually all that bad and paced in Missy's kitchen, thinking. He'd been working in Delgado's operation for years. Figuring out the place should be a no-brainer. If only he was back in Chicago, he could put this thing to bed.

Hearing an unfamiliar noise outside, he walked out onto Missy's back deck. Ron was in his yard unfolding chairs, so he walked across the grass. "Looks like the makings for a party."

Ron glanced up. "Missy didn't tell you?"

Jonas shook his head, but then he hadn't given Missy much of a chance with the way he'd been purposefully keeping his distance.

"My birthday's today and Jan wanted to celebrate. A man doesn't turn sixty-five every day, I guess."

"Would you like some help?"

"If you're offering I won't be turning you down."

"I'm all yours."

Ron set him to work setting up several banquet tables and arranging chairs. Next, he helped fill coolers with an assortment of beer, sodas and water, and then he assembled the party tent for shade. Jonas was probably pushing it a bit with all the stretching and lifting, but it felt good to be active.

After he'd finished with the obvious, he turned to Ron. "Anything else?"

"We're having it catered by Jan's coworkers at the inn, so the food's covered." Ron glanced around. "I guess there's nothing left for you to do except come on over here later on tonight and help us celebrate."

"Me? You want me to come?"

Holding Jonas's gaze, Ron said, "Why not?"

"Look, you don't know me. It's okay—"

"Missy told us who you are."

Jonas studied him. "She told you…"

"That you're her husband."

She'd told Gaia, too, which had surprised him. He'd be gone within the week, so what was the point? Maybe that's not what really bothered him about the admission. Being a husband implied a close relationship, but he was having a helluva time figuring out exactly what he was to Missy. And what she was to him.

"She told us about the Camden part of the whole deal, as well."

"She must trust you very much."

"Apparently. She knows Jan and I would do anything for her."

"She's lucky to have you."

Ron took a dark bottle from the cooler and held it out to Jonas. "Why don't you sit and chat awhile?"

Jonas hesitated, but a cold beer sounded good. He took Ron up on his offer. What followed was a round of twenty questions. Where'd you grow up? Where's your dad? Close to him? It was the exact type of interrogation any man meeting a woman's father for the first time would expect, only Ron wasn't Missy's dad and Jonas wasn't prospective suitor material. Even so, there was no doubt he was sizing up Jonas.

"Okay," Jonas said, his patience finally wearing thin. "If Missy's told you who I am and who she is, then she's no doubt told you that she wants a divorce. So what are you after, Ron?"

"Yeah, she told us. Is that what you want, too?"

"What I want doesn't matter."

Ron was silent for a moment. "You still love her, don't you?"

Jonas snapped his head up. "To be honest, I'm not sure I know what love is."

"Tricky, isn't it? Well, I'll tell you one thing. A man doesn't walk away from a woman and get away with it for four years, only to pop back into her life again for no reason."

"How I feel or don't feel about Missy doesn't make a whole lot of difference. Missy may come across as being a laid-back flower child, but once she makes up her mind about something, she's more stubborn than a mule."

"I'll tell you what I think."

Jonas hadn't asked, but he had a feeling he was going to get an earful in any case.

"I think you're the type of man who would do anything for the woman he loves. Including working night and day trying to support her. Trying to give her the life she was used to."

Jonas drained his beer.

"Sometimes a woman needs to know she's the most important thing in a man's life. And sometimes the words mean more to her than anything else."

"Maybe Missy never loved me." He stood up and tossed his bottle into the recycling bin. "Maybe she was just rebelling against her family, her dad. Ever considered that?"

Ron nodded. "For about two seconds."

"Yeah, well, she had you fooled for four years." Jonas started walking away.

"Missy's never tried to fool anyone about anything."

Jonas stopped.

"I may not know a lot about you, Jonas, but I know

Missy." He shook his head. "I remember very clearly the look on her face when she told us about you dying. It was the look of a woman who had loved her husband very much."

"You weren't there, Ron. How can you have a clue what happened?"

"Sometimes we see what we want to see. Even if it isn't the truth. Those are the times we need to put aside what we think and trust what we *know*."

"THAT CAN'T BE LAUREN and Kurt," Missy said, shaking her head. "They look so grown up."

"Sixteen," Sophie Bennett said as she watched her twin teenagers carry their twin baby brother and sister around to meet the guests at the Setterbergs' backyard party.

Lauren's hair was still long, but darker than Missy remembered and her figure had turned decidedly womanly. Kurt's hair had lost some of its babyish curl and his face and arms displayed the healthy look of a young athlete.

"Are they driving?" Missy asked.

"Oh, yeah." Noah Bennett laughed, throwing his arm around his wife's shoulder. "For the first time they were a bit reluctant to come to Mirabelle for the summer."

"I suppose that no car rule puts a damper on things."

"A little." Sophie smiled. "But they both love Mirabelle."

"Sixteen, hmm," Missy mused. "Would either of them be interested in working at Whimsy over the week of Fourth of July?" That was the busiest week of the entire tourist season and she and Gaia could no doubt use the help.

Noah and Sophie glanced at each other.

"They're both helping out Marty and Brittany at the inn," Noah explained.

"But Lauren would jump at the chance to work at your shop," Sophie added. "She gushes over your merchandise."

"Why don't you ask her," Noah suggested.

"I'll do that."

"Missy!"

Noah and Sophie meandered away as someone called her name. Missy spun around to find Natalie Steeger Quinn coming toward her. "Natalie!" She hugged her friend. "When did you get back to the island?"

Natalie lived in Minneapolis during the school months and ran a summer camp for kids on the property she inherited from her grandmother on the northwest side of Mirabelle. Though they'd e-mailed and talked by phone on occasion over the winter, nothing replaced seeing each other in person.

"A couple weeks ago, but things have been so chaotic with the baby and the new camp kids that I haven't had time to come into town. Couldn't miss this, though!"

Natalie's husband, Jamis, their baby girl tight in his arms, came toward them. "Hello, Missy."

"Hi, Jamis." She held out her arms. "Can I hold her?"

Clearly reluctant to give up his child, it took him a moment to hand her over. Missy looked into the wide, dark eyes of tiny Anna and felt her heart melt. "She's beautiful."

Jamis put his arm around Natalie's shoulder and kissed her head. "I need a beer before I face this crowd." With that he wandered over to the coolers.

"Well, he's as friendly as ever." Missy chuckled. "How's it going?"

"With all that's happened so quickly, there've been a few wrinkles to iron out." Natalie grinned. "I've never been happier than I am with Jamis."

The unlikely couple had met here on Mirabelle almost exactly one year ago, and since then, they'd adopted four kids, gotten married and gave birth to their own child. Marriage and motherhood looked as if they agreed with Natalie.

When the baby fussed and Missy's attempts at calming her failed, she handed her over to Natalie.

Natalie propped the little bundle on her shoulder and within minutes all was quiet. "What about you?" Natalie said, concerned. "I've heard a couple of unsettling rumors through the Hendersons."

Missy explained everything.

Natalie searched through the crowd. "That's him over there, isn't it?" True to form, she'd completely passed over the Camden part to focus on the husband-returning-from-the-dead part.

Jonas sipped on a beer and busied himself preparing for a campfire later in the evening. He'd stacked firewood near the fire pit and was arranging kindling inside the ring of rocks Jan and Ron had built in their backyard.

"The one true love of your life back from the dead," Natalie murmured. "What are you going to do?"

"I don't know."

"You're married. You still love him." Natalie shrugged. "Seems simple enough to me."

Leave it to Natalie to see only the positive in everything.

"Who said I still loved him?"

Natalie laughed and shook her head. "You didn't have to *say* anything."

"Not everything is as simple as it looks."

"He came back for a reason, Missy."

"When he leaves again?"

"What if he stays?"

"Fate was wrong, Natalie. It happens."

"Maybe. Then again, maybe her timing was just off by a few years."

Their timing was off? That was something Missy had never considered. What if she and Jonas had met too soon?

Natalie suddenly waved excitedly. "Sarah! It's good to see you!"

Missy held her breath as Sarah joined them. Sarah hugged Natalie and glanced at Missy, but quickly looked away. They hadn't seen or spoken to one another since the tell-all discussion in the back room of her shop.

As Sarah and Natalie caught up, Brian ran to Missy and gave her a hug. "How you doing, Bri?"

"Okay." Then he glanced at the group of kids of varying ages gathered around a table of munchies and said, "I gotta go!"

A moment or two later, the Hendersons arrived at the party and Natalie was drawn into a conversation with them. Missy and Sarah were left standing awkwardly side by side.

"Can we talk?" Missy asked.

Tentatively, Sarah glanced at her. "I'd like that."

"I hope you understand nothing I did, didn't do, said, or didn't say was meant to hurt you."

"I know that now." Sarah's eyes watered. "I probably over-reacted a bit, but…" she said, pausing to gather herself. "I'm not ready to go into the details, yet, but Brian's dad comes from a very wealthy family. Not in a Camden way, but they're rich enough to throw their weight around. And they do."

That explained a lot. Knowing her friend would share more when and if she was ready, Missy didn't push. "I'm sorry, Sarah."

"Missy, you're nothing like them, and I should've remembered that right off the bat. You have nothing to be sorry about."

Missy threw her arms around Sarah and hugged her.

"Honestly, I felt a little lost these last couple of days without you."

"You weren't the only one."

Sarah stepped back and took a deep breath. "So what's happening between you and your...husband?" She laughed. "It's just so weird to say that. I swear, it won't be long and I'll be the only single woman on Mirabelle."

CHAPTER FIFTEEN

JONAS STACKED ANOTHER ARMFUL of wood by the fire pit. If he kept at this, they'd have enough fuel here for a week's worth of fires. He glanced around the Setterbergs' backyard and inwardly cringed. It'd been years since he'd been to a party. Everywhere he looked people were laughing, talking, relaxing and having fun.

Relaxing and having fun. How did people do that, exactly?

A buffet was set up at one end of the yard with a large frosted cake covered in candles at one end, hot dogs, burgers and grilled chicken on the other end and corn on the cob, watermelon, baked beans, potato salad and various other side dishes and munchies in between. Folks wandered back and forth from the food to the coolers. They stood in groups or sat at the many tables he and Ron had set up earlier that day.

Since Missy had practically dragged him over here almost an hour ago, Jonas had kept to himself, delaying as long as possible the inevitable socializing. What he couldn't figure out was why she wanted him here in the first place.

He glanced around looking for someone he could stand next to without bothering overly much with conversation. The guy at the grill looked like a good candidate. Beer in hand, he seemed perfectly content flipping burgers and ignoring the crowd. Jonas wandered over to him. "Hey."

"Hey yourself." The guy barely glanced at him.

"Need any help there?"

"Got it covered." He took a swig off his beer. "Missy's husband, right?" Obviously, the man noticed more than he let on.

"Yeah. Jonas." To keep on the safe side, he didn't bother with his last name.

"Jamis Quinn." With a spatula in one hand and a bottle of beer in the other, he didn't offer to shake hands. "You sure caused quite a stir showing up here on Mirabelle."

"I've been away on some…long-term business."

"Sure you have."

Jonas ignored the comment. He couldn't help but notice Missy talking with a woman he'd never met and cuddling a small bundle of a baby in her arms. What was it with her and babies?

"That's my wife, Natalie," Jamis said, his gaze suddenly softening. "And Anna, our youngest."

"New baby?"

He nodded. "If I were you, I'd watch out. Baby fever's making its way around this island."

Jonas couldn't help but chuckle. The virus wasn't likely to hit Missy's house, at least not while he was still on Mirabelle. "How many kids do you have?"

"Five."

"No shit?" The guy didn't look that old.

"Four are adopted," he offered in response to Jonas's puzzled look. "Galen and Sam are my oldest." With a proud look on his face, he pointed at a couple of teenagers. "They're over there with the Bennett twins, Kurt and

Lauren. My two little ones, Toni and Ryan are there," he said, smiling and pointing at a table of younger kids. "Sitting with Garrett and Erica's nephew, Jason, and Sarah Marshik's son, Brian."

Big happy families.

Oh, hell. Now Missy was holding Garrett and Erica's baby boy. If she wanted kids so damned much why hadn't she gotten married again right after he'd died?

"I'm happy for you guys that you've decided to adopt," Jamis said. "It's been the best thing for me and Nat."

"What?"

"Adoption," Jamis said, turning a couple burgers. "Missy's—" He glanced at Jonas and immediately shut his mouth.

"Missy's adopting," Jonas murmured. That fit her.

"I'm sorry. I assumed…"

"That since I'm her husband I'd know. Don't worry about it, man."

Missy as a mother. Somehow it made so much sense. Jonas wondered if his sudden reappearance had impacted the process. Figures. One more way Jonas had screwed up her life.

The conversation turned to the mundane and several hours later, Jonas, having kept on the fringes for most of the night, finally sat silently around the blazing campfire. He would've gone back to Missy's house except for the fact that he'd found himself fascinated by watching Missy, listening to conversations and getting to know these islanders a little better.

Drinking hot cocoa, chatting and laughing, a group of about ten had remained long after the rest of the party had gone home. Someone mentioned that a place called the Draeger mansion on the outskirts of town had finally sold, and the talk turned to rumors it had been purchased by the Andersens' long lost daughter. In spite of the company, every time Jonas glanced over the flames into Missy's face and caught her gaze, it seemed as if they were completely alone in the darkness.

During a lull in the conversation, Missy pulled a small pouch out of a pocket in her fleece jacket and handed it to Ron. "Happy Birthday, Ron."

"Hey, we said no presents."

"It's not a big deal."

Ron reached inside the small, beaded fabric bag and took out a bracelet made from turquoise.

"Turquoise is a natural healing stone," Missy explained. "It's probably overkill, but I included all seven chakras stones to promote well-being. There's one for Jan, too."

Ron handed the bag to Jan.

She took out another bracelet and smiled at Missy. "They're beautiful."

"Thank you, Missy," Ron said before he and Jan exchanged looks.

Jan released a heavy sigh. "I suppose this is as good a time as any to tell them."

"What?" Sarah asked.

"Jan and I are retiring," Ron said.

The sounds of disappointment traveled around the circle, but Missy held silent, straightening her spine as if waiting for more bad news.

"We're not going anywhere, though," Ron said. "At least not for a while."

"You're not?" Missy said.

"We don't mind the winters," Jan said.

"We're just getting old," Ron explained. "Tired. We need to relax more."

"So I'm leaving my job at the Mirabelle Inn," Jan said.

"And I'm selling the equipment rental business," Ron added.

"What about the buildings you own?" someone asked.

"Oh, we'll hold on to those." Ron smiled. "I need something to do."

Jonas was glad for Missy's sake that the Setterbergs would be staying on the island. He glanced at Missy and noticed her almost sighing in relief. Jonas didn't know much about Jan, but he could imagine how the older woman's protective instincts had helped Missy feel the love she'd been wanting her entire life. Ron, though, was the father Missy had always wanted. Who wouldn't want Ron for a father?

Although Ron's comments to Jonas earlier in the day had held a distinctly parental tone, Jonas had felt amazingly comfortable with the man. *Trust what we know.* What did Jonas know?

He remembered back to the first months of his marriage to Missy. Remembered how she'd looked at him, with trust and reverence. How she'd touched him, with both tenderness and passion. Back then he'd never doubted her love for him.

So what had happened?

Unable to answer the questions turning over and over in his mind and feeling exhausted, mentally and physically, Jonas slipped away unnoticed from the fire. He went back to Missy's house and sat quietly in one corner of the deck, hiding in the shadows.

Only partially listening to the conversation continuing

by the fire at the Setterbergs', he glanced into a brilliant night sky. Suddenly, the cat jumped onto his lap. Jonas scratched his neck and the animal slowly settled down to knead his leg. The tension that had been building inside him all night left his shoulders, freeing his mind. Over and over, he went through the time he'd spent with Missy what seemed so long ago, trying to find the moment when things had begun changing between them.

The group around the fire called it a night and dispersed, and a moment later Missy came back to her yard. She stepped onto the deck. He knew the exact moment she felt his presence. For a moment, she fell completely still, and then she turned to go inside.

"Missy?" he whispered.

"I'm sorry," she said. "I didn't know you were out here."

"When did our marriage start falling apart?"

At first, she didn't say anything, but still she sat across from him. The cat jumped down from his lap and went to Missy. "I think for me," she began slowly, "it was the night you called from Los Angeles to tell me you wouldn't be back as expected. It was our six-month anniversary. Six months that we'd been married. I'd made a special dinner. Steak for you. Fish for me. Everything was out, ready to go. Your flight was supposed to have already touched down."

"I remember. I was under a lot of pressure. That was the first really big case I was in charge of."

"For me it was the first in a long string of missed dinners and weekends spent alone."

"They were watching, wanted to see what I could handle," he said. Not to mention the fact that if he'd made good with the FBI, maybe then her family—her father—would accept him. "I wanted so much for us, Missy. A home. A family. A life. I wanted to provide for you."

"And all I ever wanted was for you to be there."

"You knew the demands of my job before you married me."

"I can't argue with that. It's true." She put her head down. "I was naive, selfish. I thought...I thought *I'd* be enough. That you'd want to be with *me* more than be off on the next assignment."

"Missy, I wanted to be with you, but it was my job. The way I paid the bills, cared for you, provided for you."

"I didn't need anyone to provide for me. Not then. Not now. I can take care of myself, Jonas. All I ever wanted was to share my life with you."

His first reaction was to argue that she was being impractical again. There was no way he could've relied on her trust fund to support them, but that wasn't entirely fair. A lot of FBI agents made a decent living without the long hours. Was it possible it hadn't been her expectations alone that had driven him so hard in his job?

"I'll admit, I was immature," she went on. "Probably hard to live with, but I never set out to hurt you, Jonas."

"You filed for a divorce." She'd not only broken his heart, she'd hurt his pride. It was something he had to face and accept. What Ron had said to him suddenly struck home. *Trust what you know.* He knew Missy. She'd loved him. Something had happened. "Why? Can you finally tell me why?"

Missy looked away.

"Missy?"

"The last straw was not being able to get ahold of you, not being able to talk with you…" She paused, seemed to be gathering herself. "The day I'd had a doctor's appointment and found out that I'd…I'd had a miscarriage."

"What?" he said, not comprehending.

She glanced back at him. "I had a miscarriage."

"Miscarriage?" He stared at her. "You were pregnant?"

She nodded.

"With our child?"

Silently, she nodded.

He tried to absorb it, make sense of it. Trying to remember back to everything that had happened the days preceding her filing for a divorce. He'd gotten home from two weeks away on a tough assignment and she'd changed. He'd sensed it the moment he'd stepped inside the house.

He covered his face with his hands as images of her holding that baby at Duffy's and then tonight at Ron's party ran through his mind. She'd lost her own baby. She'd been in pain, physical, emotional and she'd suffered through it alone. "Why didn't you tell me?"

"Because you were gone. Like you were always gone. Because it hurt like hell to know whatever case you were working on was more important than me. That you would drop everything you were doing for work, but that I didn't matter."

"That isn't fair." Defense mechanisms quickly rose. "Things were different then. You were…immature and had unrealistic expectations of a husband."

"Actually, there's some truth to that." She nodded, wrapped her arms around herself. "But is it unrealistic to expect a husband to be around more often than not?"

The ramifications hit Jonas like a bus. "You never even told me you were pregnant."

"Would it have made a difference?"

He didn't know what to say, couldn't seem to find his voice. It was all too much to swallow.

She stood and headed toward the house. "That's what I thought."

CHAPTER SIXTEEN

THE NEXT MORNING, AFTER having worked all day every day since Jonas had arrived on the island, Missy lay on her side in bed with Slim curled up in front of her. Gaia was opening, so Missy didn't have to go in to Whimsy until after lunch. A brief reprieve before the hectic week of the Fourth of July was bound to do some good.

Slim stretched out a paw and gently patted her cheek, looking for attention. After scratching his neck, she was rewarded with a loud purr. "I've missed you, too." She kissed his forehead. For so long it'd been just the two of them, it seemed odd to share her house with Jonas.

She pictured Jonas leaving Mirabelle and her stomach flipped. When he first showed up she couldn't wait for him to go, and now she found herself wishing he'd stay. Apparently Jonas was more unfinished than the rest of her business.

"What do you think he'll do, Slim?" She nuzzled his neck. As if she'd gotten too close, too soon, Slim stood and stretched his way off her bed. "You, too, huh? Figures."

Marin had always loved cats.

Missy's thoughts returned to the short conversation she'd had with her sister the other day. Had she cooled down enough to call her back? Probably not. Had she talked to their father, told him about their conversation? What if her dad simply showed up one day on Mirabelle? She might be ready to face a lot of things. He wasn't one of them.

Missy tossed aside her covers, showered and dressed, but instead of following her instincts and hightailing it out of her house before Jonas roused, she hung around putzing in the kitchen and making them both breakfast.

When he wandered down the stairs a short while later in only a pair of boxers, she immediately regretted her decision. She couldn't force her gaze away from the dusting of dark hair covering his otherwise smooth, muscular chest.

He spotted her and stopped. "Morning."

"Good morning." Awkwardly, she looked away.

"Sorry." He rubbed his pec muscles and yawned. "I'd have put some clothes on if I'd known you'd be here."

"It's okay."

"I think I have some things in the dryer." He wandered into the laundry room off the kitchen.

Missy found herself watching him, taking in his strong legs flexing as he bent, pulled a clean, white T-shirt out of the dryer and tugged it over his head. He came back into the kitchen, looking rumpled with his bedhead and wrinkled clothing, but incredibly sexy. "Hope you don't mind I did a load of laundry yesterday."

All the unnatural politeness oozing from him was going to drive her crazy. Then again, he was trying to meet her on her terms. How could she fault that? "No, that's totally fine." She pulled a plate out of the oven where she'd been keeping warm a breakfast burrito, filled with scrambled eggs, peppers and hash browns, and set it on the counter. "Here."

"You made me breakfast?" He wouldn't take his eyes off her face.

"It's the least I could do after stiffing you with the dinner bill at Duffy's the other night."

He chuckled, sat at the counter and pulled the plate toward him. "This smells great." He picked up his fork and paused. "Missy?"

She held her breath.

"I'm sorry you went through a miscarriage alone. I can't even imagine how you must've felt." He gave her a small, tentative smile. "For what it's worth, a baby might've turned the tide for me."

"Meaning you would've never taken that undercover assignment? You would've stayed?"

"Absolutely. I could've never walked away from that responsibility."

A responsibility. That's all a baby would've been to him. So what was she? "I gotta run. Have to do a few more things at my store before opening up."

Jonas held her gaze. Clearly, there was more he wanted to say, but she couldn't bear to be around him just now. "Have a good day," he whispered.

Her hands shaking, she took off out the front door. The moment she reached the porch, she closed her eyes and took a deep breath.

"Missy!" It was Ron calling from the sidewalk. "You coming, or what?"

"Yep. I'm coming." Doing her best to put Jonas out of her mind, she caught up with Ron. They talked about Ron's party for a few blocks. When they reached the back door of her gift shop, she invited Ron inside. "I have a surprise for you." She unlocked the alley door and stepped back to let Ron inside.

"Well, I'll be a son of a gun," he said, looking around

at all the free space and organized shelves. "Honestly, Missy, I didn't think you had it in you."

"I don't." She laughed. "Jonas did this. He helped me out front, too." She followed him, waiting for his reaction.

"Mmm-mmm-mmm," he said, shaking his head. "This looks great. It's like a whole new store. How does it feel?"

"Good. Great."

He winked at her and then said, teasingly, "Maybe you oughta think about keeping that man of yours around for a little while longer."

"Yeah. Right." Then her smile dimmed. "What is it with men and responsibility?"

He cocked his head at her.

"Jonas," she explained. "All I am to him is an added responsibility."

Ron chuckled. "Oh, I'm quite sure you're more than that to him."

"Nope." She shook her head.

"Missy, honey, other than…" he said, pausing and fumbling a bit. "Other than, you know…sex, nothing says love better to a man than bringing home a paycheck, or fixing a leaky faucet." He pointed at the shelving in her back room. "Or cleaning a storeroom."

Missy glanced around as Ron slipped out the back door. Was it as simple as that? Jonas wanting to take care of her? As she was puzzling through Ron's comments, her cell phone rang. On picking it up, she glanced at the display. Barbara. This was it. She could no longer avoid the inevitable. "Hi, Barbara."

"So we haven't chatted yet about Jessica's surprise visit. I have to tell you, she was so pleased to meet you. Said she felt an instantaneous connection. I think this is going to work."

"I'm not so sure." Missy took a deep breath and accepted this wasn't the first time Fate had been wrong about her life. "There's something I need to tell you."

For more times than she wanted to count, Missy explained about Jonas. Barbara never said a word, no questions, no comments, no guttural sounds of disbelief. By the time Missy got to the end of the story, her apprehension about the adoption had escalated to foreboding. Under no circumstances was she going to use her real family name and money to smooth over this situation. If she couldn't adopt a child on her own, so be it.

"If I'd known you and Jessie were planning on coming to the island, I would've mentioned this sooner," Missy finished. "Really, nothing's changed. At least not—"

"I'm sorry, Missy," Barbara interrupted. "I'm afraid everything has changed."

Missy held her breath.

"Jessica has been adamant throughout this entire process that a divorce is an automatic disqualification. Her parents divorced when she was young and she doesn't want that for her child."

"What if Jonas and I don't get divorced? What if we stay together?"

There was a long moment of silence. "I'm not sure I can, in good conscience, recommend you to Jessica. Under the circumstances."

"I understand," Missy whispered.

"Call me when the dust settles, dear, and we'll start over again. Your match is out there somewhere."

THE MOMENT MISSY WALKED through the front door later that night, Jonas knew something was wrong. Sorrow furrowed her brow. She only glanced toward where he sat on the couch and wouldn't maintain eye contact. She didn't even make a comment about the cat jumping down from his lap to greet her and barely noticed as he weaved in and out around her ankles.

"Hey," he said, glancing at the clock. "You're home early."

She turned to set her keys on the counter, and he would've sworn the sudden brightness in her eyes was the pooling of tears. There was only one other instance he remembered her being this sad. When she'd asked him for a divorce. The cat meowed at her and she picked him up, nuzzled his neck.

He wanted to kick himself, but the urge to go to her and put his arms around her in comfort overwhelmed him. While he wouldn't allow that to happen, he didn't need to be an unfeeling ass. "You used to hate cats," he said softly, hoping he could gently urge her into talking about what was bothering her.

A lopsided smiled touched her mouth. "I did."

"So how'd he come into your life?"

"Now there's a story." She came into the living room and dropped onto one of the chairs not far from him. "Only a few days after your funeral, I hit the road to no particular place. Stopped at motels whenever and wherever I felt like it. About a week into it, I stopped at this motel, got a room and then proceeded to clean the garbage out of my car. Went back to the Dumpster to throw everything away. Just before I closed the lid, I heard the tiniest of mews coming from under all the garbage."

"Damn," he muttered.

"I pulled stuff out left and right. Then I saw this plastic bag. Squirming. Barely. I found him inside. Sick. Malnourished. Eyes bulging out of his head. His four brothers and sisters inside the bag were already dead." A tear dropped from her lash and immediately he regretted the topic of conversation. She looked at him and smiled. "Before that day, I'd never taken care of anything. I was having a hard enough time taking care of me."

"But you did it."

"He was so sickly for such a long time the vets didn't think he was going to make it, but I made it my mission to nurse that tiny lump of matted fur back to health. Now look at him. You'd never know he was such a runt."

He'd turned into such a beautiful, healthy cat it was hard to imagine anyone had once upon a time literally thrown him away. "You never have told me his name."

"Slim." She chuckled. "Slim chance of survival. That's what the vet told me. He used to love cruising in the car with me. He'd wrap himself behind my neck all slim and sleek and look out the window. The breeze blowing in his face."

Jonas could easily picture it. Missy and her cat against the world.

"I saved his life," she whispered. "In return he saved my soul." Another tear dribbled down her cheek.

"Whatever is bothering you, Miss, I'd like to help."

She opened her mouth as if she might lean on him, and then quickly stood and shut him out. "Nothing important. Bad day at work. I'll be fine." Then she walked back into her bedroom, closing off the tentative connection between them as surely as if she'd slammed a door in his face.

Jonas wavered for a long moment. He had no right to interfere in her business, but had he become the kind of man who couldn't give without taking? Not quite.

Walking down the hall, he knocked. "Missy?" He could hear her trying to stifle her tears.

She looked up when he opened the door and his heart nearly broke. She'd changed into a T-shirt and knit shorts. Sitting on the bed, she brushed away the tears trailing down her face, but there was no point. As soon as she swiped her cheeks dry, more tears replaced the others.

He sat on the edge of the bed and, setting aside his promise to keep his hands off her, pulled her into his arms. "This is about you wanting to adopt, isn't it?"

Her body shook. "You know about that?"

"A little. Jamis told me at Ron's party."

Between broken sobs and ragged breaths, she explained all she'd gone through over the past several years in her quest for a family. It didn't sound as much like a process as an ordeal.

"You want—ache—for a family. Maybe because you've turned your back on your own."

She glanced at him, as if he'd hit a chord she didn't know existed.

"I know you have your reasons, and they're good ones," he said. He'd always felt as if his presence had only widened the gap between Missy and her family. If he could help her repair the bonds, maybe then he could forgive at least a part of the damage he'd caused. "Maybe you should reconnect at least with your brothers and sisters."

"I tried. I called Marin the other day."

"And?"

"She hung up on me."

Her tears gathered again in earnest.

"Give her some time. If she misses you as much as you miss her, I'll bet she'll be calling you back." He paused and tightened his hold on her. "If she doesn't, though, remember that you're not alone, Miss. You've made a family here on Mirabelle. They all love you very much."

"I know. It's just that a child would complete things, I think."

"Me reappearing threw a wringer in everything, didn't it?"

She didn't have to say anything for him to know he was right. If he'd known then what he knew now, he wouldn't have come to Mirabelle.

"I'm sorry, Missy." The apology didn't begin to cut it, but it was all he had. There was no making this right. All he could do was lie back on the bed and hold her, help her feel better if only for a while.

SLIM HOPPED ONTO THE BED. Missy awoke abruptly and froze. The room was dark, but for light from a sliver moon glowing through her open window. Several hours had clearly passed since she'd come home. The cat moved tentatively, sniffing the quilt, her toes and Jonas's leg. Then he, amazingly accepting of this large addition to a space that had previously been reserved only for him, curled in the crook behind Jonas's knees and proceeded to clean the day off his fur.

The air was cool, cold even, but the heat of Jonas's large body had kept her warm. He was tucked at Missy's back, so close she could barely move. His arm thrown around her, his hand resting near her breasts, his lips at the nape of her neck. His breath teased her skin with slow, even strokes. It was one of the most perfect moments Missy could remember. Most of the perfect moments in her life involved Jonas. But then most of her completely heart-wrenchingly devastating moments had involved him, too. Because they were so closely tied together. Because he meant so much to her. Because she loved him.

She still loved him.

She should've known her feelings for him wouldn't change all that much. She'd put a piece of her heart to sleep, she supposed, but Jonas coming back had reawakened her with a vengeance. The brash, young love she'd first felt for Jonas had matured and grown into something so much deeper, headier and complete because *she'd* matured and grown. Given another chance, she would never be so quick to throw away what they'd had.

Drawing his hand to her mouth, she softly kissed the pad of his thumb. He tensed behind her. She brought his hand to her breast, felt her nipple harden against his palm. He groaned, as his fingers closed over her breast and his mouth pressed against her neck.

Then she turned to face him, dipped her hands under his shirt, splayed her fingers through the springy hair on his chest, and kissed him. As she slipped her tongue between his lips, he shuddered with need.

Instinct took hold as he dragged her shirt upward and cupped her breast. Arcing against him, she threw her leg over his hip, reached lower between them and closed her hand around his erection.

He jerked and pulled away. "Missy, don't," he whispered. "You don't—"

"Shh," she whispered, touching his lips. "What if…what if we tried again?"

"Tried what again?"

"Our marriage. What if we—"

"No." He sat and ran his hands through his short hair. "It's over."

Taking his face between her hands, she made him look at her. "We've never been over, Jonas, and you know it. I want to give us another shot. I want to work things out—"

"You want a family. That's all, Miss." He drew her hands away. "You don't want me."

"That's not true. I want a family *with* you."

He went to the door. "You want what I can't give."

"How do you know until you try?"

"Been there, done that. Remember? We failed."

"Then why did you come back?"

He stared at her. "To be honest, I'm not sure anymore. In any case, it was a mistake."

Losing Jonas once had nearly crippled Missy. As he walked away, she didn't know how she'd survive losing him again.

JONAS LAY IN BED STARING AT his laptop bag. The divorce agreement was still in there. For Missy's sake, he should sign it and move on. He'd been pushing his luck staying on Mirabelle this long. Rather than give himself the option of backing down, he rolled out of bed, took the papers out and signed them. Done. Then he carried them downstairs.

Though the sun was only now rising on the horizon, he found Missy sitting at the kitchen counter with various types of stone beads splashed before her. Intent on her project, she wasn't aware of his presence. Carefully, as if only one particular color or shape would do, she selected one bead after another and slipped it onto a leather cord.

Once she'd apparently reached an acceptable length, she finished it off by tying some kind of a clasp on each end. Then she sat back, placed her hands over the piece of jewelry, and closed her eyes, apparently blessing the piece.

Her focus and patience amazed Jonas. Sitting that quietly with that type of a project would've been nothing less than torture for him. He well remembered what it had felt like to be the sole object of her attention, and there'd been no better feeling in the world. Whether she was giving a back rub, trying out a new recipe for dinner, having a conversation or making love, when Missy chose to do something, she did it with complete abandon, immersing her entire self in the task at hand.

It was one of the many things he'd admired about her. She was so different from him with her carefree ways and, yet, no less disciplined. Why in the world would a woman like her, with so much to give, want to give their marriage another go? It didn't make sense. He couldn't offer her anything.

Resigned, he finished his descent. "Morning."

Startled, she glanced up. "Morning."

He smiled, trying to keep things light between them. "Is that a blessing or a curse you just put on that bracelet?"

"Blessing," she whispered. "It's silly, I know, but it can't hurt, right?"

"Do you make all the jewelry that you sell at your store?"

"Only some of it."

"You go through that process for every piece?"

"No." She shook her head. "That would be too time-consuming."

"So this is for someone you know?"

"It's for you."

Oh, hell.

She pointed to the various small round stones. "Turquoise to heal. Hematite to ground and focus. Onyx to keep you safe." She stood and walked toward him. "For your health, to help your wound heal. To ground your thoughts and energies so you can solve this case."

"The sooner I leave the better? Well, then, it's a good thing I already signed this." He set the divorce agreement on the counter.

She glanced at it, but said nothing, only fastened the bracelet she'd made on his wrist and walked away.

He ran his hands over the smooth stones and felt them still holding the warmth of her skin. God help him, but he wanted her warmth on him. "Missy?"

She stopped, turned and waited.

He could find no words to explain how he felt.

"If only I could make something to heal a broken heart," she murmured before disappearing out the door.

Hers or his?

CHAPTER SEVENTEEN

MISSY COULD FEEL JONAS slipping away from her just as he had four years ago, and just like four years ago she was helpless to stop him. The only difference between then and now was the woman she'd become wasn't going to look for an easy way out. She was going to fight for what she wanted, for Jonas.

This morning, though, he needed time to absorb the changes happening between them, and she needed to give him space to do just that. She left the house early, wanting to get to Whimsy to prepare for what had proven to be the busiest day of the summer season for all the shops on Mirabelle, the day before the Fourth of July.

Her cell phone rang on her walk to her shop. Without looking at the display, she answered. "Hello."

"Melissa?"

Missy quickly sat on the nearest curbside bench. "Marin!"

"I'm sorry I hung up on you the other day. I guess your call threw me. I needed some time to think. Put things in perspective."

"I get it."

"I need to know something." Her sister paused. "Tell me why? Can you explain to me why you felt it was necessary to disappear?"

"That's been hard for a lot of people to understand." Marin would. At least, Missy hoped she would. "I never fit with the family, remember? I'm different from all of you. You know that."

"That's a good enough reason to take off for years?"

"Marin, I needed to be away from all of you in order to be able to find me. Dad would never let me be me. Jonas's funeral was the last straw."

"Why? What happened?"

She told Marin about what their father had said at the funeral.

"Dad's a pain in the ass," she interrupted. "I understand that more than you know. Don't you think I haven't had issues with him?"

"You have?"

"Damn right. He's controlling and opinionated. He thinks he's an expert on everything. You know that. He's always telling me how to run my career, and it drives me crazy."

"But, Marin, you've always been able to stand up to him. You're so much stronger than I am."

"Not really. I disagree with him. I argue with him. But I'm no stronger than you, Mel. Your strength might be quieter than mine, but it's there."

Missy felt tears gather in her eyes. "I don't know what you're talking about."

"I remember watching you, my little sister, standing there with that serene smile on your face taking everything Dad was throwing out at you. I used to get so angry at him, for berating you and you for taking it. Then one day, I was home for Christmas break. You were a freshman in college and he was dictating what you'd be majoring in and what classes you needed to take when he pulled the old 'Or, by golly, I'm all done paying for tuition.' And you, as calm as all get out, looked at him and said, 'Then don't pay.'" Marin paused. "Mel, you were the one who taught me how to stand up to him."

A tear dropped from her lashes and then another one as Missy remembered that day as if it had been yesterday. It was the day she realized she could not be around her father if she ever had a hope of discovering what she wanted in life. It was the day she realized she had to leave her family behind. Now she could admit to herself that it'd been painful to leave her siblings, painful to leave even her mother. That's probably why it had taken her a long while to take that step.

"If I was so strong, Marin, why couldn't I figure out a way to be myself even around Dad?"

"I don't know. Maybe now you can."

Missy didn't know what to say.

"I'd like you to try, anyway. You're the only sister I will ever have in this world. I'd like to think we've all grown a bit and can tolerate our differences, maybe even learn to respect one another."

"You think?"

"I'd like to try. I'd like to see you."

"I'm not sure I'm ready to do that. At least not yet. Did you tell Dad we talked?"

"No." She paused. "I thought about it. I was mad. Even picked up the phone and dialed his office number, but I guess a part of me understands. I did let Mom know you were alive and okay—"

"She'll tell Dad—"

"She won't. She's different than you remember her. Can I at least give her your phone number?"

Missy scratched her head. "You know—"

"Fine. Have it your way—"

"Don't, Marin! Don't hang up again! You don't understand what's going on here. I can't be found right now by anyone. Especially not by Dad. You know she's never been able to keep a secret from him."

"What's going on?"

"It's too long a story, and I'm sure you don't—"

"I do care, Mel."

She tipped her head back trying to hold off more tears. "I do miss you, Marin. Someday, soon…"

"What can I do to help?"

She explained Jonas's situation. "So if Dad finds out where I am, he might inadvertently alert the wrong people."

"So where do we go from here, then?"

With that one question, Missy felt another cog in the gears of her life move into place.

MISSY WAS WALKING BACK from a quick lunch break at the park with Sarah. The store was crazy busy, but Lauren Bennett had agreed to help out this week, so Gaia wasn't alone. They were only a block from their shops when they passed the Hendersons' drugstore.

"Oh, wait!" Sarah stopped. "I ran out of tape. I need to see what they have here before I head back to my shop." Sarah dashed inside.

Missy followed her and meandered up and down the aisles while waiting. She passed a row of diapers, then baby formula and glanced at the cute pictures of infants plastered on the products. When she reached the feminine supply section, she paused as a strange feeling swept over her. Her menstrual cycle was late. That rarely happ—

It'd been…she calculated…two weeks and a day since she and Jonas had made love. Hope leaped to life inside her. A baby. She grinned even as tears gathered in her eyes. Jonas's child. Their child. Glancing at the boxes of pregnancy tests, she knew she would have no peace until she knew for sure. She snatched up a couple boxes and was in the process of paying for them when Sarah reached her side.

"All set. You ready to—"

Missy quickly stuffed the boxes into a bag. "Yep, let's get out of here."

The moment they stepped outside, Sarah whispered, "You've had sex with him? I thought you hated the man."

"So did I. Turns out I still love him."

"You think you're pregnant?"

"I don't know."

"Oh, my God," Sarah murmured. "You can't go back to your store with those. Come with me." She dragged Missy through the front of her flower shop and toward the small half bath in her back room.

Missy closed the door. Her hands shook as she withdrew the pregnancy test. Several minutes later, having followed the directions, she sat on the closed toilet seat, her head in her hands.

"Well?" Sarah asked through the door. "Do you know?"

Missy opened the door, and showed Sarah the stick.

"Wow," Sarah murmured. "Just wow."

Missy was pregnant with Jonas's baby. Pregnant.

Oh, God. Elation warred with fear. She wanted this baby, almost as much as she wanted Jonas, but what if she miscarried again? What if her body couldn't make a child? The first miscarriage had been bad enough, knowing her marriage was failing and, yet, believing that a baby would pull them back together. When those dreams were shattered by the miscarriage, she'd lost all hope for her and Jonas. How could she go through that again? Losing both Jonas and their baby?

"I have to make sure." Missy closed herself in the bathroom again and went through another test. Pregnant again. She opened the door.

"What are you going to do?" Sarah whispered, her face displaying every possible emotion.

Missy smiled and held back tears. "I didn't plan this, but I want this baby. More than you can know."

"Are you going to tell him?"

"I don't know."

THAT AFTERNOON WORKING at Whimsy dragged by in a haze for Missy, despite the fact that business had been so brisk she'd barely left the cash register. More than once, she'd thought to take the last few hours off so that she could go home and confront Jonas, but she couldn't leave Gaia and Lauren alone that long. Besides, she had no clue what she'd say to him. By the time Gaia left and she closed her shop, she was a mass of nerves, but she knew what she had to do.

Pregnant or not, she wanted her marriage with Jonas to work. As far as she was concerned, divorce was no longer an option. Pulling out the divorce decree Jonas and she had both signed, she ripped it up. Piece by piece, she tossed it into the shredder.

This meant she was going to have to tell Jonas about the baby. Eventually. What if she lost this baby, too? Then what?

Snapping open her cell phone, she dialed, jiggling her legs impatiently while waiting for the answering machine to finish. "Sean," she said. "I need a favor."

Half an hour later, Missy nervously waited in his private office, Sean having opened the medical clinic just for her. She was pacing back and forth in front of his window when the door opened and Sean stepped inside.

"Well." He held her gaze. "You're definitely pregnant."

She covered her mouth. "You're sure?"

"As sure as any doctor can be."

"Would you be able to hear a heartbeat?"

"It's too early for that, Missy." He shook his head. "That's normal. There's nothing to worry about."

"I had a miscarriage several years ago," she explained, wrapping her arms around herself. "I never did hear a heartbeat."

"I'm sorry." Then he went through all the statistics that she'd heard a million times over about how often miscarriages happen. "First pregnancies are the most common to miscarry. Just because you lost the first one, doesn't mean you will the second."

"Is there any way for you to know…"

"All that I can tell you is that based on the tests your hormone levels are very strong. That's a good sign." He took her hand and drew her down the hallway. "Come on. I'll take you home."

They went outside and walked in companionable silence for several blocks. "Are you going to tell Jonas?" Sean asked.

She hesitated. "Not yet." He'd said a baby would've changed things for him, but only because of the added responsibility.

"Missy—"

"A baby won't change anything for him. Not really." Only create, in his mind, a responsibility to stay. "If he stays, I want him to stay for the right reasons."

"Are you sure he's leaving?"

"Yes. Absolutely. As soon as he figures out this case he's been working on, my life may very well go on as before."

"You think?"

She looked away. No. Nothing would be as it was before. They reached her house and stopped on the sidewalk.

"You know I'll be there for you, right?" Sean said. "No matter what happens with Jonas." Before she could say anything, Sean cupped her face and gave her a soft, incredibly sweet kiss. His touch did not cause a wave, let alone a ripple, of awareness inside her.

He pulled back and smiled. "I should've known," he whispered. "But I had to try."

She reached up and touched his cheek. "I'm sorry, Sean." She might be confused about a lot of things and still trying to completely figure out who she was inside. But there was something she was becoming more and more sure about with each passing moment. She would always be Jonas's wife. He would always be her husband.

"Well, for what it's worth, Missy, you helped me feel at least something again. It's been a very long time."

She touched his arm. "I don't want to lose you as a friend."

"That's not going to happen."

"If you ever want to talk…"

"I'll probably have to go through Jonas to get to you."

JONAS SAT IN THE SHADOWS on the porch and watched the doctor take Missy's hand. He caressed her knuckles with his thumb. Jonas felt every single touch like a punch to his gut, and still he couldn't look away.

He didn't have to hear a single word of what they were saying to one another to know what was passing between them. The tender smiles. The way they leaned toward each other. The way they looked into each other's eyes. Then it happened. That man held Missy's face in his hands and kissed her. Slowly. Gently. Sweetly.

Rage, the likes of which Jonas had never known, surged through him. It was all he could do to breathe. What did Missy think she was doing kissing another man? Who did that doctor think he was to kiss another man's wife?

Wife.

And who the hell was Jonas trying to kid?

He looked away as the anger he felt turned inward. He'd left his *wife* high and dry. He had no rights to her body, soul or future. She could do as she pleased, and apparently Sean Griffin pleased her. Not Jonas.

He stood and forced himself to watch the intimate exchange between Missy and Sean as they stood on the boardwalk, moonlight shining down on them. So that's what she wanted? Tenderness? Jonas didn't have a gentle bone in his body. He no longer knew how to be soft, kind, forgiving.

It was time he admitted that he'd been less than a stellar husband. She'd married him, loved him, given herself to him in the only way Missy knew how to give, completely and with total abandon. All she'd wanted in return was for him to love her back, to be there. He hadn't been. At least not enough. He'd put work above Missy, day in and day out. He'd taken from her too much, never given enough of himself.

With one last smile for Missy, the doctor turned and walked down the sidewalk. Missy watched him for a moment before coming up the path toward the house. Her sandaled foot hit the porch and, as if sensing his presence, she turned.

"Jonas. Why are you sitting out here?"

"Waiting for you," he whispered, his voice suddenly raspy.

"I was just…" She trailed off.

"You don't owe me an explanation." He walked toward her.

"No. I don't."

He stopped before her and looked into her beautiful green eyes, wanted with everything in him to reach out and caress her face, but he didn't have a right. Not now.

It hadn't been Missy's expectations that had driven him on. It'd been the ones he'd set for himself that had done the most damage. Whether it had been his pride spurring him on in his career, or his pain in believing he would never be enough for her, it hadn't mattered. The results had been the same. He'd broken Missy's heart. This time, he was going to make his leaving easy on her.

"I'm sorry, Missy." He looked straight into her eyes. "I'm sorry I wasn't there for you. I'm sorry I didn't do a very good job of showing you how much you meant to me. Sorry for all the pain I've caused you. During our marriage. Faking my death. And now. Bringing it all back. Truly. I am sorry."

She stared at him, her mouth slack, very likely in shock. When had he ever apologized to her and meant it?

"I don't understand. Why are you doing this now?"

He stepped back out of reach so that he wouldn't try to touch her. "Because you asked for more from me and I never gave it to you. Because I never shared in the blame in things going wrong between us. You deserve someone like your doctor. Someone who can give you more." He slipped past her toward the steps. "It's time for me to move on." Now, for her sake, he had to leave. "You deserve better than me, Miss."

CHAPTER EIGHTEEN

DUMBFOUNDED, MISSY WATCHED Jonas walk away. His head bent in concentration, he charged quickly down the hill and was out of sight in no time. Presumably, he'd been sitting on the porch and had seen Sean kiss her. So why the apology? Why not an angry, jealous outbreak?

Confused and feeling more than a little raw, she walked into her house. Too tired to think, she readied for bed before climbing between the cool sheets. Unfortunately, sleep failed her. Could it be that Jonas finally and truly was taking responsibility for his part in their failed marriage? Then why was he walking away?

More than an hour later, still awake, she heard him at the front door. Quietly, he went upstairs.

Let it be. Let him leave. Let him go.

She couldn't. Already, her heart was breaking just imagining what it would be like to go through each day without him. Missy climbed out of bed and tiptoed to his room. Dressed only in boxers, he was waiting for her at his bedroom door, his gun drawn. "I heard movement," he explained.

Always, always working.

"I didn't know it was you," he said softly, putting the gun down.

"I couldn't sleep."

His gaze wandered for a moment over her silky camisole before snapping back to her face. The furrow on his brow intensified. "Go back to your own bed, Missy."

"What if I don't want to?" She stepped forward, reached toward him. "What if I—"

"Don't." He grabbed her wrist and held her away from him. "Don't ruin what you've got going with Sean. Not for me. I'm not worth it."

"See that's the thing. There's nothing going on between me and Sean. Never has been. Never will be."

Assessing what she said, he studied her.

"We thought about it, I suppose," she explained. "Both of us. From the beginning. Before you came to Mirabelle. There's nothing between us, but friendship. He and I both know that."

"He kissed you."

"He wanted to know if there could be anything. There isn't. What you saw was a goodbye of sorts. We're friends. That's all."

She pulled one of her hands out of his grasp and touched his cheek, making him look at her. "After I thought you'd died, my life was never the same. I realized what I'd lost. I regretted more than you can imagine not finding some way to make things work between us. Because I knew I'd never find that kind of love again."

"We had some fun, didn't we?" he said. "But what we had wasn't enough."

"Things are different today, Jonas."

"You have a chance to move on. Without being a widow. Take it."

"There won't be any moving on for me. Ever. Because I still love my husband."

"Missy." He looked away. "You don't know what you're saying—"

"I do." She pressed her hands flat against his hard chest. "I know what I'm saying. I know what I'm doing. I know what I want."

"You're too good, Miss. Too whole. Too free and forgiving. Too rich. Too smart. Too everything. And me? I haven't changed. It didn't work before. It's not going to work now."

"Put me first more often than not. Love me. That's all you have to do."

"I'm not sure I'm capable of giving you what you need, Missy. What you deserve. Even if I could figure it out, it's still…I can't…it's the job…you know what it's like. I—"

"There's never been any other man for me, Jonas. There never will be."

"Then you're a fool."

"Am I?" She wrapped her hands around his neck and kissed him. "A fool for wanting this?" she murmured against his lips.

He closed his eyes and groaned. "Don't."

When she kissed him again, his mouth opened to her. He'd proven that she belonged to him. Tonight she was going to turn the tables. Before this night was over, he was going to know in no uncertain terms that he belonged to her.

She pushed him back onto the bed and pulled off his boxers. His erection pulsed into the air. When she slowly, deliberately drew her camisole over her head, he looked away, clearly trying to maintain control.

"This isn't going to solve anything."

"I don't care. I want this. I want you." She stepped out of her silky bottoms and climbed over him, straddling him.

His erection pressed against her flesh and she moved back and forth, caressing him.

Right then and there, she wanted nothing more than to take him inside, but rather than controlling, this was about surrendering, accepting the inevitable. She wanted him to know what he'd be giving up if he chose to leave her again.

She covered his mouth with a kiss so deep and slow that when he groaned again, the sound vibrated through her. She kneaded his chest, kissed his neck, his shoulder, his flat, muscled abdomen, and then held his penis and took him into her mouth.

He sucked in a breath and pressed his hands flat against the mattress, refusing to touch her. "Don't," he breathed. "Don't do this."

Over and over, she gripped him, loved him, gave to him. Soon, his entire body was shaking and his control broke. He bracketed her face with his hands and pushed her away from him. Looking into his eyes, she climbed higher and poised herself over his erection, daring him to roll away from her.

Slowly, she pressed down and took him inside.

"Missy." He pulsed against her. "Obviously, I'm the one who could never say no to you." Then, giving in to the inevitable, he trailed his fingers along her throat and cupped her breasts.

The breath rushed out of her as he squeezed both nipples. "I love you," she whispered, rocking against him.

In one swift and smooth movement, he gripped her shoulders and rolled them over. She was under him, her legs spread, rejoicing in the feel of his weight on her, moving against her.

He lifted her hands above her head and ran his palms

along the underside of her arms, stopping at each of her seven tattoos. Then he buried his face in her hair, kissed her neck, bit her earlobe.

"Smelling you has always been like opening the door and coming home," he said softly, trailing kisses down her neck. He moved across her collarbone, along her chest and finally took her nipple into his warm mouth. "Tasting you somehow eases every hunger I've ever known."

"Oh…Jonas," she said, groaning and cupping his tight, muscular backside.

Then he grabbed her hands, entwined his fingers with hers, held her down and looked into her eyes as he entered and retreated over and over. This time was everything the sex they'd shared weeks ago hadn't been, and it was clear that the intimacy they'd experienced so many years ago was stronger than ever.

She pulsed with him, moved instinctively. He felt the same, but different. Bigger, stronger, but more gentle. At once infinitely better and yet comfortably familiar.

"Not a day went by these past years without me thinking of you, Missy, wanting you, wishing things had been different."

"Things can be different." She looked into his eyes and rose to meet him with every thrust. "Stay with me. Don't ever leave me again."

For the moment she let herself believe it was possible, let herself hope they might have a future together. A future as loving parents to this baby inside her. The moment was only her and Jonas, joined together, loving one another as if tomorrow might never come. As if they could both stay lost on Mirabelle for the rest of their lives.

She clenched his hands and arched to meet him one last

time before her body let go in the most cataclysmic release she'd ever known. He came inside her only seconds later, and the world and all its troubles dissolved between them. They were only a husband and wife loving one another in the best way they knew how.

THE DISTANT, CLEAR SOUND of a loon's lonely cry came through the window on a cool breeze. Jonas lay awake in bed facing Missy with only a sheet covering them.

Whether she was awake or not was debatable. Though a contented smile graced her lips, her eyelids had grown heavy. Suddenly, she stretched, throwing her arm above her head.

He brushed each one of the Sanskrit letters tattooed on the underside of her arm with his fingertips. "You don't need chakras symbols to ground you, you know. You're doing just fine all on your own."

"That's what I thought until you showed up on my doorstep."

"I'm sorry, Missy."

"Don't be. The more the dust settles, the more I realize you coming back into my life was the best thing that could've ever happened to me."

"Or you've gotten good at lying to yourself."

"Jonas. You're a good man. You were a good husband. Things fell apart between us simply because we met before we were both ready. Fate wasn't wrong. Our timing was off."

"That's what you think?"

"That's what I know."

"And now?"

"Now is our time. The right time." She curled into him and kissed his chest. "I don't want you to leave."

He'd be no better a husband today than he'd been all

those years ago, but suddenly, on the verge of losing her again, he wondered what it would be like to build a family, a life with Missy here on Mirabelle. In the end, though, he knew he couldn't be what she needed.

"I've pressed my luck long enough," he said, accepting the inevitable. "I need to leave here before I put anyone in danger. Stein's got to be brought down. The only way that's going to happen is for me to face the music. I have to go to D.C., Miss."

"Not tomorrow. Stay one more day?"

For what? One more day would only make what he had to do all the more difficult. "It won't change anything. I still have to go."

"Stay for me. Please. It's July Fourth."

She was stalling with any excuse she could find, but he didn't have the heart to force it. "One more day." He wrapped his arms around her and in no time her shoulders rose and fell in the slow rhythm of a peaceful sleep.

He, on the other hand, wouldn't be getting much sleep tonight, not with what he'd just done weighing on his mind. Even after he'd sworn to make his leaving easier on her, all he'd done was make this harder by making love to her, by making her think this is the life they could have. What man could've resisted that look in her eyes, the way her skin looked in the moonlight? The feel of her. The smell of her.

He buried his face in her hair and breathed her in.

Home. Peace. Contentment. And if he just let go…love.

She still loved him. After everything he'd done to her, after how he'd treated her, how could that be?

And him? He was incapable of giving her what she so freely gave to him. He was only going to hurt her again. All the anger he'd felt over her wanting a divorce was long gone.

She deserved a husband one hundred percent of the time. She deserved someone who could always put her first. She deserved a man who could love her. That man wasn't him.

"GOT HER!" THE VOICE SOUNDED loud over the cell phone. "She's on a little island on Lake Superior. Mirabelle."

"Finally!" Mason breathed a huge sigh of relief. "Wisconsin?"

"Yep."

"And?"

"You were right. He's with her. I'm watching the house as we speak."

This is it. Stein took one last look around his Arlington home. A week from now, he'd be in Samoa or Tonga. Maybe Thailand. He grabbed his Glock and his jacket and took off out the door. "I'm on my way."

"They're both asleep. I can get this over and done with, Mason. Right now."

"She's a United States senator's daughter, for God's sake. You can't just make her disappear."

"I don't care if she's a princess. I don't want any loose ends."

Mason ran a hand over his tired, dry eyes. "All I'm saying is that you can be sure there will be a thorough inquiry."

"By which time, we'll be long gone."

"Don't make a move until I get there."

There was a short pause. "Then you'd better get here fast."

CHAPTER NINETEEN

SINCE SETTLING ON MIRABELLE, July Fourth had become Missy's favorite holiday. Sunshine and heat, sweet treats and fireworks, who could ask for more? The islanders always did Independence Day up right with a morning parade followed by a 5-K run. After those activities, there were kayak and windsurfing races, a sailing regatta, free music in the town square and a watermelon eating contest. Last, but by far not least, were the evening fish fries, corn boils and bonfires by the shore followed by fireworks over the water.

Missy let Gaia manage the gift shop, promising to pay her and Lauren double time for working, and had taken the entire holiday off. Unfortunately, Jonas was so preoccupied that by the time evening rolled around, Missy was almost wishing she'd gone to work.

After spending most of the afternoon wandering down Main, from the pier all the way around through town and out to the Mirabelle Island Inn via Island Drive, they'd ended on the beach walking through the sand.

Jonas studied the groups of people scattered here and there. Though he was wearing sunglasses, Missy knew from the tense set of his jaw that he was working.

"Hey." She touched his arm, and he immediately covered her hand with his own. The gesture was so comfortable, so intimate, she almost blurted out, "I'm pregnant," but it wasn't the right moment. She wasn't sure there ever would be a right time. "What's the matter?" she asked.

"This day is making me nervous." He continued to eye the crowd and studied the boats gathering offshore in preparation for viewing the fireworks over the water. "They could be here. On the island. The crowds are so thick...."

"Did you see someone you're worried about?"

"No."

She may have talked Jonas into staying one more day, but she could tell by his preoccupation she'd only delayed the inevitable. One way or another, he'd be leaving tomorrow. Somehow, someway, she would find a way to live in Jonas's life alongside his job. "You should know something," she said, taking his hand.

He glanced at her.

"I ripped up the divorce agreement. You want a divorce, you'll have to get one yourself."

JONAS HATED CROWDS. THE HEAT, noise and rudeness were bad enough without having to rub shoulders with strangers and stand in interminable lines. For what? A crappy hotdog and a warm beer. But he would've gone through the day all over again just to see the way the firelight from the bonfire at the water's edge illuminated Missy's face.

"What?" she whispered, catching him studying her.

"Nothing." He looked away to watch the yachts out on the water. What would it feel like to own one of those boats? To not have a care in the world? To not have to worry anymore about putting the bad guys behind bars? To enjoy life?

"The fireworks should be starting any minute." She grabbed his hand and pulled him to an open grassy area. "Do you want to sit over here?"

No, he did not want to be a sitting duck. He wanted to be up against the retaining wall, their backs covered, but there wasn't an inch of space available.

"Jonas?"

"All right." He let himself get tugged down next to her.

Something about the sight of those yachts anchored just offshore bothered him. He'd never thought of the possibility of anyone coming at him from the water. As soon as dusk settled and the sky turned black, she shivered.

"Cold?"

"A little."

"No sweatshirt, jacket or blanket." He moved behind her, tucking her against his chest. "All I got is me," he whispered in her ear.

"You'll do," she said, a smile in her voice as she dropped her head back to rest against him.

It was his first moment of complete contentment all day. Maybe he could get used to this. Maybe she was right by dropping the whole divorce thing. Maybe he should try and make it work. And maybe all he'd succeed in doing was breaking her heart all over again.

What he refused to think about was the impact on his own heart. With every passing minute, getting on that ferry in the morning was sounding more and more problematic.

Why do you have to go? Suddenly the reasons seemed unclear. She wanted him. He wanted to stay. What more was there? For starters, he had to finish this assignment before resolving anything with Missy.

They'd no sooner settled together on the ground than a

succession of loud, ear-popping, chest-beating booms went off, followed by a bright and massive explosion in the sky, illuminating the boats on the water.

The boats. Yachts, too.

Yachts. That was it! Delgado's yacht. With a helicopter pad, it was the safest place for the deal. He had to call Reynolds, ASAP. Just then, he noticed something—someone—in his peripheral vision. Someone moving differently. Eyes in the crowd watching. Someone alone. A predatory presence. Another boom sounded and he stiffened. It was too noisy, too dark and too crowded. This was a very, very bad idea.

"We need to leave." Abruptly, he stood, grabbed Missy's hand and pulled her back through the crowd.

"Wait a minute!" She pulled her arm away from him. "The fireworks just started."

"Too bad."

She tugged against him, holding her ground. "You've been on edge all day. Tell me what's going on, or I'm not moving."

He glanced over her head, studied the crowd surrounding them. "Missy, I'm not messing around here."

"Then quit trying to protect me and tell me what's happening."

He looked into her eyes. She was right. He'd been treating her like someone who couldn't handle the truth, and if there's one thing he'd learned about Missy these past few weeks it was that she could handle about anything. "I didn't want to mention it, but…"

"What?"

"Someone's here," he whispered in her ear. "Watching us. Following us. I can feel it. One minute I glimpse a face, eyes following us, and the next it's lost in the crowd. It's more of a feeling than anything. I don't trust this night. This crowd. Something doesn't feel right."

"That's all I needed to know. Let's go."

Once they crossed Main and headed up the hill, the crowd all but disappeared. A few locals were in their front yards, sitting in lawn chairs watching the fireworks display, but the streets were empty. By the time they reached her house, his instincts were on high alert. He climbed the porch steps. Missy reached for the door first. He stilled her hand. "Let me go in first."

"Do you really think someone's here?"

"Better safe than sorry." His gun drawn, he took the keys out of her hand, opened her front door and slowly stepped inside. The feather he'd placed on the top of the frame floated silently to the floor. "Stay here." He went to the back door and found that door, as well, undisturbed. "We're good," he called and went into the living area.

That's when he noticed his laptop. He caught Missy's gaze and signaled for her to keep silent. "Stay there," he mouthed. One room after another, he cleared the house, including every closet and the basement. Then he flipped on the TV and drew her into the bathroom. "Someone was here," he whispered. "Using my computer."

"How do you know?"

"The pencil. I always place it lead facing upward. It's possible they've bugged your house. I'm gonna guess they're waiting to make a move until they find out how much I know and who I've told."

"So what do we do?"

"*We* don't do anything." He looked into her eyes, and knew he'd never forgive himself if something happened to

her. He should've never stayed on the island this long. "*I*
have to leave Mirabelle. Right now."

"Stay. Talk to Garrett. He'll help."

"This is my problem. I can't risk anyone on the island
getting hurt. Me leaving is the only option." He left the
bathroom, climbed the steps and packed his bag.

When he turned, she was standing at the door.

He put a finger to his mouth. They couldn't talk out here.
He took her hand and led her back into the bathroom.

The moment the door closed, she pleaded quietly, "Take
me with you."

The look on her face nearly tore his heart apart. He
cupped her cheeks in his hands. "No."

"I lost you once." She placed her hands softly on his
chest. "I don't want to lose you again."

He kissed her, hard, rested his head against her forehead.

"Promise, you'll be back," she whispered.

"I promise." Whatever she needed to hear, he'd say it.
"I have to go." The sooner he got off Mirabelle, the sooner
the threat to Missy would be gone. He turned to leave.

"Jonas?" She held the door closed. "There's something
you need to know."

He waited.

"I meant what I said last night. I love you."

He dropped his bag and pulled her into his arms. "It's
going to be okay, Miss." He rested his chin on her head.
"I've been in worse spots before." He wasn't sure that was
true, but there was no point in worrying her.

"I'm pregnant."

He went still. *Pregnant.* He could feel her heart racing
against his chest and in no time his own body picked up
the beat. "How…? Oh, God. That first night." He looked

away. The night he'd gone to her room, found her naked in the moonlight and unfairly seduced her. "Obviously."

"I wasn't going to tell you." She pulled away. "I don't want to hold you here if it's not where you want to be."

He didn't know what to say. He wasn't sure he could be the husband she deserved; how could he be the father this child would need? "Missy—"

"You don't need to say anything. Or do anything. I know you have to go."

He held her gaze, trying desperately to accept that she was carrying his child. His baby. He reached out and pressed his hand to her stomach. Their child.

"I want you to come back, Jonas." A tear slipped down her cheek as she covered his hand. "Just come back alive, okay?"

"I'm not—"

"Come back, or I'll be coming after you."

He nodded and knowing he couldn't waste another moment, took off out the door. On his way down the hill any number of things he could've—should've—said ran through his mind.

I want this baby. I want you.

That's when it hit him. *Missy, I love you. Never stopped loving you.*

What if he never got another chance to tell her? What if—

His cell phone rang and he flipped it open.

"You can run, but you can't hide."

Stein. Jonas shot off the street and ducked behind a massive oak tree. "Let's take this off the island, Stein. I don't want any civilians getting hurt."

"Too late for that. You have something I want. I gave you the chance to turn it over, but you had other ideas. You left me no choice."

"Where are you?"

"Now I've got something you want."

Jonas held his breath, hoping against hope that he was wrong.

"Your wife."

No! No, no, no.

"Jonas!" Missy screamed in the background. "Leave! Get off—" The line went dead.

CHAPTER TWENTY

HE HAD MISSY. THE BASTARD was dead.

Jonas raced toward Missy's house, his thoughts erratic as panic overtook him. Then he stopped as a spark of reason filtered through impulse. Stein wouldn't be working alone. He was too smart for that. That meant there'd be at least one other man with Stein and Jonas's handgun wasn't going to cut it.

Running back down the hill, he found the police station closed. After breaking the window, he climbed inside and quickly, methodically searched for their weapons stock. A false door hidden in the back of a closet in the chief's office seemed the most likely option. He busted it down to find a locked cabinet. After shooting off the lock, he yanked open the doors.

The handguns here, too, were worthless to him in this situation. He was happy to see a semiautomatic, and snapped it up along with several clips, some tear gas and a couple of sets of cuffs.

"Going somewhere?" A man's voice came from behind him.

Jonas spun around to find the police chief, Garrett Taylor, his weapon drawn and pointing right at Jonas's head. "This isn't what it looks like," Jonas said.

"Looks pretty straightforward to me. A man I don't know from Adam is stealing weapons."

"I'm an FBI agent. Special Agent Jonas Abel."

"Badge?"

"It's at Missy's. We don't have time for this. They've got her."

"Who?"

"Missy." He sucked in a breath. "My wife!" Neither time, distance, nor divorce papers would ever change that. She would always be his wife. Always. And he would always, always be her husband.

Keeping his gun trained on him, Taylor backed up to the phone on his desk. "All I've heard is rumors. Give me a minute to verify your story and then we'll go."

Seconds ticked by. The reality of the situation bore down on Jonas and his hands shook. "Missy doesn't have time for this." He started toward the door.

"Take another step and I'll shoot."

Jonas held the cop's gaze. "Then you better make damned sure you kill me." He walked straight past Taylor, knowing every step might be his last.

"Wait."

Jonas stopped.

"You're going to need some help."

"No offense," Jonas said, turning. "These are FBI agents gone bad. They're heavily trained, move very fast and have nothing to lose."

"Well, I got a lot to lose." Taylor scooped up another semiautomatic and headed toward him. "So I guess I'll just have to move faster."

As they ran out of the station and climbed the hill toward Missy's house, Jonas filled Taylor in on what he knew of the situation. "One man will be inside, one out. It'll be a trap and they'll use Missy for bait. It's me they want. You got a choice between saving me or Missy—"

"Let's hope it doesn't come to that."

"But it might. Don't let anything happen to her."

"Like I said before. You, I don't know from Adam. Missy is a good friend of mine."

"Good. That's good."

On silent agreement, they approached Missy's yard from the neighbor's. Every shade, blind or curtain in Missy's house had been drawn, and every light was on. Whoever was inside was ready to receive anything that hit him.

"You cover the woods out back," Jonas ordered. "I'm going in. I could use a diversion." Without a radio, they had no way to silently communicate.

"How long do you need to get in position?"

Jonas glanced into the trees. "Three minutes from when I hit the roof."

"That should be enough time for me to locate the man guarding the perimeter. When I do, I'll make some noise."

He glanced at Taylor. The man looked and acted capable, but this was life or death. Possibly Missy's. "You sure you can handle—"

"Fifteen years on the Chicago P.D. oughta be good for something," Taylor said, interrupting. "I chose Mirabelle. She didn't choose me."

"All right, then." Jonas strapped his gun over his neck and climbed the oak tree in the yard bordering Missy's. Thirty feet up he traversed a branch that looked sturdy enough to carry him to the massive elm in Missy's yard.

Channeling featherlight weight he went as far out on the oak limb as he dared and then jumped. On catching the targeted elm branch, he heard it crack with his weight. Quickly, as the branch dipped lower and lower, threatening to give way, he made it toward the center of the tree. Lowering himself to the roof of Missy's house, he quietly moved to the dormer of her guest bedroom, carefully knocked out a pane of glass and slipped inside. So far so good.

He marked the time, moved down the hall and glanced downstairs. It was as he'd expected, but the sight of Missy gagged and bound to a chair in the middle of the living room still sent a rush of rage through him like nothing he'd ever felt. Missy spotted him at the top of the stairs. Her eyes widened for an instant, but she covered her reaction well.

Good girl. Now where are they?

As if reading his thoughts, she signaled with her eyes toward the kitchen. That meant he'd have cover for only a few feet in his descent to the first floor. Carefully, he eased his weight onto the first step, then the second and down as far as he could go without making a sound or becoming visible to Stein.

Glancing around the corner, he found Stein, gun in hand, pacing in the kitchen, close enough to the steps that Jonas could get to him. The man might be management, but he was still in tip-top shape. Not wanting to risk Missy getting caught in the cross fire, Jonas would have to take Stein without his weapon.

"Webster, you clear?" Stein whispered into his earpiece and waited for the response. "Good."

Webster—ex-Special Agent Webster—had gotten fired some years back after a federal witness under his protection had managed to get killed a little too easily. Taylor was going to have his hands full outside.

Jonas glanced at his watch. Thirty more seconds. He

waited. Waited, some more. He glanced into Missy's eyes and every second felt like a lifetime. She was crying. Tears streamed across her cheek as she watched him. A short shake of her head.

Don't come down here. Don't do this.

"It'll be okay," he mouthed. "Shh."

God, how he wanted to hold her. Reassure her. Make this all go away. If he could, he would simply walk away from everything, including his job and the Bureau, and disappear with Missy. He couldn't believe it had taken him this long to see it, that it'd taken her being tied up and gagged for the truth to sink into his thick skull and even thicker-skinned heart. She was the only thing that mattered anymore in his life. He loved her, had always loved her. Without Missy life meant nothing, and *that* was the real reason he'd taken that undercover job years ago.

"I love you," he mouthed, causing an answering flood of tears in her eyes. *I'm going to spend the rest of my life proving it.*

A gunshot sounded outside, snapping Jonas back. The short burst of sound was enough to get Stein distracted and looking out the window. "Is he here?" he yelled into his mike. "Talk to me! Did you nail him?"

Jonas jumped the remaining steps and barreled full throttle into Stein, dislodging his earpiece and sending them both flying into the wall. Everything else happened in seconds. Jonas gripped Stein's wrist and knocked the gun out of his hand. Stein twisted away and went on the offensive. Jonas took a couple jabs to his gut, and then turned and punched Stein a couple of times. He grabbed him and flipped him onto the ground. Kneed him and twisted his arms behind his back.

"You're done!" he shouted, cuffing him. He would've loved nothing better in that moment than to put a bullet between Stein's eyes. Not tonight. There was someone more important. Jonas quickly went to Missy and worked off the gag.

"Outside!" she said. "They're outside, too."

"I know." Though he didn't have the time to tell her everything that was going through his mind, he tried to tell her with his eyes, the touch of his hand. "Are you okay?"

She nodded. The moment he untied her from the chair, she flew into his arms. "Let's finish this." He gave his handgun to Missy. "Shoot the bastard if he moves." Then he went to the window and cautiously glanced toward the tree line.

Taylor was walking toward the house, using a hand-cuffed and limping Webster as cover. Jonas flung open the back door, grabbed Webster and pushed him down next to Stein.

"Jonas, that's not all," Missy said, frantic. "There are three of them."

"What?"

"Matthews is outside."

"Missy, Brent Matthews is dead."

"No," Missy cried. "I saw him. I know it was him."

"Drop it, Jonas," came the sound of a man's very familiar voice behind them.

Jonas spun around to find Matthews, his undercover partner, standing in the doorway, his gun drawn and pointing at Jonas's head. "I saw you take two bullets," Jonas said. "Back in Chicago."

"Ain't Kevlar amazing? You should know better than believing everything you see."

Taylor made a slow, easy movement toward the kitchen counter.

"Don't try anything stupid, cop," Matthews said, "or Jonas is dead. You'll be next."

Taylor froze.

"Get over here by your friends."

Garrett moved toward Jonas and Missy.

"Get these cuffs off!" Stein yelled.

"I don't think so." Matthews chuckled. "I got a couple million, yours and mine, in an offshore account that says you look mighty fine just the way you are."

"You're a dead man, Matthews," Stein muttered.

"Promises, promises." Matthews kicked Stein in the gut. "Now where's that memory stick, Jonas?"

"It's too late, Brent. Kensington's got everything."

"I figured as much." He shrugged. "But Delgado doesn't know that yet."

Jonas had no illusions about this situation. The moment Matthews had what he wanted, they'd all be dead. "Why are you doing this?" he asked, stalling. *Think. Think. There's got to be a way out.*

"Isn't it always about the money?"

"So that's it? You took this assignment to finagle out some hush money?"

"Didn't start out that way." He shook his head. "Stein here was the one always looking for a bribe. But funny things happen when a man's undercover for a long time. When he's lost connection to the real world."

Jonas understood, probably too well. If it hadn't been for Missy, there was no telling what might've happened to him.

"I stopped giving a shit," Matthews went on. "So when Stein realized he needed help to make this thing happen, I didn't hesitate. We'd have brought you in, too, Jonas, if I'd have thought for a second you'd consider it, but you and I both know you're a company man all the way."

Not anymore. Now all Jonas wanted was out. Legitimately. While a life with Missy might be too much to ask, he couldn't let anything happen to her. He had to stop this, right here. Right now. For Missy's sake.

"All right," Jonas said. "Let's get this over and done with." He glanced at Missy. One last look. If he was lucky he'd have time enough to put one shot in Matthews. "I love you," he said.

A new rush of tears flowed down her cheeks as if she knew exactly what he had planned. "I know," she whispered.

Jonas bolted for the gun on the kitchen counter, redirecting the weapons fire away from Taylor and Missy.

Matthews aimed.

"No!" Missy propelled herself into action and flew through the air as Matthews fired at Jonas.

Then everything was a blur.

Missy on the ground. Blood all over. Taylor kicked the gun out of Matthews's hand. "You came to the wrong island, asshole!" he yelled before pummeling Matthews.

Jonas flew to Missy's side. "Missy!" Matthews had hit an artery in her leg. She was bleeding out. "Oh, God. Oh, God. Please." He couldn't lose her. Could never, ever live without her again. "Don't move, Miss. It's going to be all right."

Quickly grabbing the scarf Stein had used to gag her, Jonas wrapped it around her leg and tightened it as best he could. Then he picked her up. Already, she was pale.

"I got this!" Taylor called out as he cuffed Matthews. "Get her to the doc's house down the street!" He relayed the house number. "I'll send the ambulance there and call for the medical response helicopter from the mainland."

Carrying Missy in his arms, Jonas raced outside, praying like hell Sean was home.

"The baby," she whispered. "Our baby."

"Shh. Everything's going to be fine."

"I love you, Jonas," she murmured before her eyes closed and her head lolled back lifelessly.

"You're not going to die!" he called, running as fast as he could. "You can't die!"

SIRENS. LIGHTS FLASHING. Jostling motion. Making her nauseous. Loud sounds. Cold. So, so cold. Scared. *Jonas, where are you? Jonas!*

"I'm here, Miss." His warm breath in her ear. "Hold on, honey."

So tired.

"She's lost a lot of blood," someone said. Sean?

Whispers. Distant. Quiet. Real? Imagined?

"She's pregnant."

"I know…possible…kind of trauma…can cause hemorrhagic shock."

No. No, no, no.

Our baby, she wanted to cry. *Save our baby, Jonas.*

She was too tired to open her eyes, hadn't the strength to make a sound. Then there was no sound at all, only the feeling of Jonas's hand gripping hers as if he'd never let go.

CHAPTER TWENTY-ONE

"YOU CALLED IT," LOUIS Reynolds said. "Delgado, full complement of henchmen, took his yacht out this morning."

"That's where it's going to happen." Jonas sighed, glad to put this assignment to rest. By the end of the day, Delgado would be in jail along with Matthews and Stein, but he had his doubts the two FBI agent traitors would even make it to trial alive.

"All the warrants have been issued," Louis added. "We're moving on this today, the moment the deal takes place. Kensington wants you in on the operation. He's sending a chopper for you."

Jonas stood in the hospital hallway tightly gripping his cell phone. He glanced inside the room and studied Missy's unconscious face. Though she'd spent several hours in surgery and all had gone well, she still hadn't opened her eyes. Her skin was as pale as the ashy paint on the wall, and it could possibly take days for her to regain any amount of energy. The doctors had told him he could head off to Chicago and most likely be back before she'd be coherent enough to notice he was gone.

Like that was ever going to happen.

"Tell Kensington I appreciate the consideration," Jonas said. "You guys have to do this without me."

"Man, this case took the last four years of your life. You telling me you're not going to be there to wrap it up?"

Four years of living and breathing one assignment, planning day and night how to put those assholes away. Now the day was here. "Yeah, that's what I'm telling you, Louis. I won't be there."

"Staying with Missy?"

"Yep." He couldn't take his eyes off her face.

"I don't get it. She's okay, isn't she?"

"Yeah, she'll be fine." Physically. She'd lost a lot of blood, but thanks to Sean for quickly stabilizing her she was going to walk away from this mess no worse for the wear. For the most part.

"Then what's the—"

"I need to…no, make that…*want* to be here, Louis, when she wakes up." Even now, ten feet from her seemed too far away. He wanted her hand in his so he could feel her warm skin. He needed to hear the blip of her slow, steady heartbeat on the monitor to reassure him he wasn't going to lose her.

"This is going to piss off Kensington," Louis said.

"Like I give a shit?" Jonas could think of a million worse things than getting fired from the Bureau.

"I take it this means you and Missy won't be divorcing."

"Not if I have anything to say about it."

"I envy you, man. A life is a good thing to have."

"Round 'em up, Louis."

"Will do."

Jonas shut off his phone and slowly walked back into Missy's room. Ron and Jan Setterberg sat in chairs on one side of Missy's bed. He gave them both an encouraging pat on the shoulder and threw a blanket over Sarah's prone form. She'd finally fallen asleep on a cot the hospital staff had provided for Jonas. Then he sat in his chair on the other side of the bed, took Missy's hand and pressed his lips to her palm.

Much to his surprise, Jan stood and rounded the bed to come behind him. She put her hands on his shoulders, rubbed them good and hard, and then leaned over to whisper in his ear. "You're a good man, Jonas Abel."

He reached up and squeezed Jan's fingers. Everything was finally so damned clear to him. There was no place he needed to be, nothing more important, than right here, right now.

Missy was everything, and he would never doubt that again.

MISSY SLOWLY ROUSED TO the sound of raised voices in the hall.

"You are *not* coming in this room," Jonas said.

"Who do you think you're talking to?" She had no clue who belonged to that masculine voice. Then again…

She cracked open her eyes to find herself in a dark hospital room, catheters in her arms, a heart monitor on her finger, bags of unidentified fluids hanging over her head. Her tongue felt thick, her mouth as dry as a dust ball.

"I'm talking to a man who puts his pants on one leg at a time. Just like me," Jonas said. *Her dad. Go for it, Jonas.* "She doesn't want you here. She's made that perfectly clear."

Immediately, her thoughts flew to the baby. Had she lost this one, too? *Please God, no.* "Jonas?" she rasped, her voice scratchy with dryness.

Like a dream, he materialized by her side. "Hey, there," he whispered. Looking as if he hadn't shaved, let alone slept for days, he reached for her hand. "You're going to be all right." He smoothed back the hair from her face. "Want some water?"

She nodded, and he grabbed a plastic cup from the bed stand and bent the straw to her lips. After taking a long sip, she licked her cracking lips. He set the cup down, and she squeezed his hand with what little strength she possessed.

"Melissa?" The authoritative voice sounded from the direction of the door.

Glancing toward the sound, she found her father, looking so much older than she remembered, standing just inside the room. Years may have passed since she'd last seen him, but he'd lost none of his commanding presence.

Missy glanced past him to her mother. She'd changed so much. She'd stopped coloring her hair and had grown it out in a soft, shoulder-length bob. Gray was taking over, highlighting her once naturally blond hair.

"Why are you here?" she asked, more of her father than her mother.

"Angelica, don't you think it's best you wait in the hall?" her father suggested.

"No, Arthur." Not bothering to look at her husband, Missy's mother brushed past him. "It's best for me to be where Melissa wants me to be." Holding Missy's gaze, she came to stand beside the bed. "I thought we'd lost you for good this time." A tear slipped from her lower lashes.

Missy put herself in her mother's shoes and imagined what it must have felt like for her to lose a child. With how Missy had been affected by a miscarriage, it was quite possible she'd cracked, if not broken, her mother's heart. "Hi, Mom."

"Oh, Melissa." She sat in the chair next to the bed and reached for Missy's hand.

Missy didn't have the energy to pull away, even if she'd wanted to. "How have you been?"

"Never mind about me. We've missed you."

Missy nodded. That at least was a start.

Another woman slowly appeared near the periphery of Missy's vision. Dressed in a black suit and a crisp white blouse and with her hair coifed in an updated, but professional, chin-length cut, she looked as if she'd just stepped off Wall Street. "I came as soon as I heard," she said.

"Marin?" Missy's vision glazed with tears.

"Hey." Her sister leaned down and kissed Missy's cheek, brushed a piece of hair off her forehead. "Artie and Max are on their way. Is that okay?"

"Sure." Missy nodded. It'd be good to see her two brothers again. "But I'm not making any promises."

"You don't have to. They just want to see you."

"Melissa?" her father said.

Her mother and Marin were one thing. Her father quite another. "I'm not ready for you, Dad."

Jonas stepped in between her father and Missy's bed. "Okay, that's enough for now," he said. "You guys need to leave."

"But—"

"Leave."

"Dad," Marin said, grabbing his arm. "Let's go."

With a small smile and a last look filled with emotion, Missy's mother stood. "Arthur, Marin's right. Melissa needs to rest."

"If she wants to see you when she's feeling better, you can come back. Only if you promise to be nice…Senator Camden." Jonas shut the door the moment they'd reached the hallway and came back to her bedside. "Ron, Jan and

Sarah went to get something to eat. They'll be back in a few minutes."

She nodded. It would be good to see them.

"There's someone else here who wants to see you." He lifted a soft-sided carrier onto her bed. A tiny mew sounded from behind a mesh window.

"You brought Slim for me." Her eyes misted as she poked her finger inside the bag and scratched the cat's black furry forehead.

"He seemed lost without you."

She glanced up at Jonas. "Shouldn't you be with Louis Reynolds? Busting that big drug dealer?"

Settling the carrier beside her, so she could reach Slim whenever she wanted, he held her gaze. "They'll manage without me."

He didn't want to leave her. As she looked into his solemn eyes, she knew the answer to the question that had been running through her mind. "Oh, God, no," she cried, unable to stop a flood of tears.

He squeezed her hands. "There was nothing they could do, Miss."

Again. Her throat closed as reality took hold. She'd miscarried again. She'd lost their baby.

He pulled her into his arms and let her cry. Once again, all hope for them seemed lost. She'd wanted this baby so much. For her. For him, too. When every tear seemed shed, he pulled back a bit and rested his forehead against hers. "I know you probably don't want to hear this right now. There is a bright side."

"What? Now you can leave me with a clear conscience?"

"I deserved that." Jonas let loose a sigh.

"I wanted that baby, Jonas. More than anything."

"I know, but listen. The bullet that hit you, hit an artery in your leg. Sean said you miscarried because of all the blood you'd lost."

"So if I hadn't gotten shot…" She closed her eyes and more tears surfaced.

"Missy," he whispered. As best he could with all the tubes coming out of her, he pulled her into his arms and held her. "It means we can try again."

She pulled back. "You want to try?"

"Absolutely, I want to stay. With you. On Mirabelle. In D.C. Hell, in Timbuktu. I don't care. Wherever you are, I want to be."

She had to ask. "What if I can't have children?"

"Being a dad is something I've never thought much about." He paused, squeezed her hand. "These days, it's sounding…and feeling right. Adoption works for me. You've already started that process. It should be a piece of cake. But if it's not, kids or no kids, Miss, the most important thing to me is being with you."

"Forever?"

"And ever." He kissed her cheek.

She sniffled. "You're just saying that because I took a bullet for you."

"Yeah, you did, didn't you?" He chuckled. "Flew pretty damned fast, too, into the line of fire." Then he sobered, swallowed back what looked an awful lot like tears. "Don't ever do that again."

They still had issues to work out, but one thing had been settled. Neither of them would be looking for a quick way out when the going got rough. Tears puddled in her eyes. "I couldn't stand the thought of losing you again, of you dying for real."

"So you really did cry at my funeral," he whispered. "Didn't you?"

"Buckets."

He drew her hand up and kissed her fingers. "I love you, Miss. Bullet or no bullet. You're the one true love of my life, remember?" He held out his hand, palm toward her.

She reached up and placed her own palm against his, matching their love lines. "How could I ever forget?"

EPILOGUE

JONAS SAT BACK, SIPPED ON a mug of hot cocoa laced with peppermint schnapps, and enjoyed the heat of the roaring fire at his back as he listened to the banter going on around him.

"Time's up."

"That's not fair."

"You making up rules as you go?"

Ron and Jan Setterberg. Herman Stotz and his wife, Crystal. Sarah, Hannah and Sean. All had become fast friends in the last five months. Even Sean.

Garrett and Erica Taylor had invited a small group of islanders to their house for a Christmas dinner for which Erica had pulled out all the stops. Lasagna. Risotto. Two different baked fish dishes, one in a creamy savory sauce, the other tomato based with onions and fresh herbs, along with a capon and a variety of vegetables and salads. Cured meats, cheeses and olives. Pound cake, cookies and home-made candies. And an assortment of breads from sweet to crusty that would make any mouth water.

Jonas was so full he had a feeling he wouldn't need to put another single thing in his mouth for a week. "Do you eat like this all the time?" he asked Garrett.

"Why do you think I have to work out so much?" Garrett

said, chuckling. He leaned toward Jonas and added, "Herman's talking about retiring. I could use a good deputy."

"Deputy, my ass." Jonas snorted. "Better watch out or I'll take your job."

"I'd like to see you try."

They both knew Jonas was quite content working as a consultant to the Bureau and the DEA, flying to D.C. once a month for meetings. Though he'd set up an office in Missy's—their—house and managed to keep himself plenty busy, life on Mirabelle was proving to be peaceful in a way Jonas had never expected. Hell, he never even carried his gun around any longer. Kensington had told him several times his job would be waiting for him should he change his mind, but there was no chance of that ever happening.

He glanced at Missy and watched her laugh as she bent toward Sarah. Nope. No chance in hell. These days any job change for Jonas would more than likely involve downriggers and a captain's license. In fact, he had his eye on a nice-sized boat for sale in Bayfield and it wouldn't take much of his savings to start up a charter operation. FBI agent or captain, it didn't matter. Not anymore.

Missy put a hand on the slight bulge of baby at her waist and Jonas swallowed as emotion overtook him. Every single ultrasound had shown a healthy baby girl. Missy still worried something might go wrong. Jonas knew, in his gut, their little girl was going to be just fine. Men had intuition, too, he'd had to remind her.

The sound of a baby crying came through the monitor sitting on the kitchen counter.

"Not ours," Erica said.

"Certainly not mine," Sarah said, laughing.

Jonas glanced at Missy and smiled. "Ours. I'll get him." He went to the guest bedroom near the back of the log home, bent down and picked up his newborn baby boy.

Jessie, the young woman from Duluth, dissatisfied with every other prospective parent had, upon hearing their entire story, insisted on meeting Jonas. One more visit to Mirabelle and she'd asked Missy and Jonas to adopt her child. They'd no sooner signed all the paperwork than they found themselves pregnant to boot.

"Shh, shh." Jonas patted his son's back. The baby quickly quieted, but Jonas stayed in the room, enjoying this one-on-one time with his son. He kissed his soft cheek and looked in those big, dark eyes. "Sweet dreams," he murmured.

Missy came into the room and wrapped an arm around Jonas's waist. "For a man who thought himself incapable of love, you're sure doing an awfully good job."

"You think?"

"I know." She kissed him, nipped at his lower lip.

He dipped his tongue softly inside her mouth and felt the stirrings of arousal. After all these months, he would've thought his need for her would've been satisfied to some degree. Instead, it'd only grown stronger. He loved looking at her naked. All those amazing curves. That beautiful swell in her tummy. "Let's go home," he groaned, cradling the baby in his arms.

"We just started a game. It's—"

"I have a better game in mind." He nuzzled her neck, knowing it would send the appropriate shivers down her spine. "In front of our own fire."

"Are there cards involved?"

"No."

"Dice?"

"Absolutely not."

"Mmm," she moaned and leaned into him. "Now you have me interested."

Loud laughter suddenly erupted from out in the great room and someone called out, "We can hear you in there!"

"Sex fiends!"

"Get a room!"

Jonas glanced up. "How the—?"

Grinning, Missy snapped off the baby monitor. "Nosy lot, aren't they?"

Jonas chuckled. "Yeah, but I like 'em."

She sobered, then ran a hand over his cheek. "Are you happy?"

"Perfectly." He turned his face and kissed her palm.

"Sure you won't ever regret leaving the Bureau?"

"Positive."

"What if I told you I wanted to move closer to my parents, so our kids could be closer to my mom as well as my brothers and sister?"

No mention of her father. In time, maybe that, too, would come. Maybe someday soon he'd even come to terms with his own father. "I'd say your wish is my command."

"We could use some of my trust fund money to buy a house in D.C.," she suggested. "Split our time between there and here. What do you think?"

She no longer felt the need to prove anything to anyone by not spending her trust fund money, and he'd given up feeling threatened by her wealth. Their respective bank balances no longer seemed to matter.

"Missy, I don't care where we go or what you do with

your money as long as I'm a part of the equation." He put his hand on her stomach and kissed her slowly. "It's our time."

"And timing," she whispered, "is everything."

* * * * *

*Be sure to look for Helen Brenna's
next Superromance, a sequel to her
October 2008 book—FINDING MR. RIGHT.
Available in November 2010,
wherever Harlequin books are sold.*

HARLEQUIN®
Super Romance®

COMING NEXT MONTH

Available June 29, 2010

HARLEQUIN®

A *Romance*

FOR EVERY MOOD™

Spotlight on

— Heart & Home —

Heartwarming romances
where love can happen
right when you least expect it.

See the next page to enjoy a sneak peek
from Silhouette Special Edition®,
a Heart and Home series.

*Introducing McFARLANE'S PERFECT BRIDE
by USA TODAY bestselling author Christine Rimmer,
from Silhouette Special Edition®.*

Entranced. Captivated. Enchanted.

Connor sat across the table from Tori Jones and couldn't help thinking that those words exactly described what effect the small-town schoolteacher had on him. He might as well stop trying to tell himself he wasn't interested. He was powerfully drawn to her.

Clearly, he should have dated more when he was younger.

There had been a couple of other women since Jennifer had walked out on him. But he had never been entranced. Or captivated. Or enchanted.

Until now.

He wanted her—*her,* Tori Jones, in particular. Not just someone suitably attractive and well-bred, as Jennifer had been. Not just someone sophisticated, sexually exciting and discreet, which pretty much described the two women he'd dated after his marriage crashed and burned.

It came to him that he…he *liked* this woman. And that was new to him. He liked her quick wit, her wisdom and her big heart. He liked the passion in her voice when she talked about things she believed in.

He liked *her.* And suddenly it mattered all out of proportion that she might like him, too.

Was he losing it? He couldn't help but wonder. Was he cracking under the strain—of the soured economy, the McFarlane House setbacks, his divorce, the scary changes in his son? Of the changes he'd decided he needed to make in his life and himself?

Strangely, right then, on his first date with Tori Jones, he didn't care if he just might be going over the edge. He was having a great time—having *fun*, of all things—and he didn't want it to end.

Is Connor finally able to admit his feelings to Tori, and are they reciprocated?
Find out in McFARLANE'S PERFECT BRIDE
by USA TODAY bestselling author Christine Rimmer.
Available July 2010,
only from Silhouette Special Edition®.

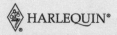

HARLEQUIN®

Showcase

LESLIE KELLY
Naturally Naughty
Wicked & Willing

On sale June 8

Reader favorites from the most talented voices in romance

Save $1.00 on the purchase of 1 or more Harlequin® Showcase books.

SAVE $1.00 on the purchase of 1 or more Harlequin® Showcase books.

Coupon expires November 30, 2010. Redeemable at participating retail outlets.
Limit one coupon per customer. Valid in the U.S.A. and Canada only.

52609057

5 65373 00076 2 (8100)0 11654

Canadian Retailers: Harlequin Enterprises Limited will pay the face value of this coupon plus 10.25¢ if submitted by customer for this product only. Any other use constitutes fraud. Coupon is nonassignable. Void if taxed, prohibited or restricted by law. Consumer must pay any government taxes. Void if copied. Nielsen Clearing House ("NCH") customers submit coupons and proof of sales to Harlequin Enterprises Limited, P.O. Box 3000, Saint John, NB E2L 4L3, Canada. Non-NCH retailer—for reimbursement submit coupons and proof of sales directly to Harlequin Enterprises Limited, Retail Marketing Department, 225 Duncan Mill Rd., Don Mills, ON M3B 3K9, Canada.

U.S. Retailers: Harlequin Enterprises Limited will pay the face value of this coupon plus 8¢ if submitted by customer for this product only. Any other use constitutes fraud. Coupon is nonassignable. Void if taxed, prohibited or restricted by law. Consumer must pay any government taxes. Void if copied. For reimbursement submit coupons and proof of sales directly to Harlequin Enterprises Limited, P.O. Box 880478, El Paso, TX 88588-0478, U.S.A. Cash value 1/100 cents.

HSCCOUP0610